VALENTINE JOY

"Wh-what are you doing here?' Amelia asked.

"I-I came for a bath." He flushed. "I mean . . . the butler spilt . . ."

"Spilt tea on you?" Amelia asked, her eyes lighting. She gave a small laugh. "He did on me as well."

"I-I better leave."

"No!" Amelia exclaimed.

"What?" Michael asked.

"I mean," Amelia said, an enchanting flush covering her, "I-I am finished here. And I am sure you will want a bath. *I* shall leave." Amelia moved toward the edge of the bathing pool and grabbed up a large, white bathing sheet which rested upon the side. "If-if you could turn around, please."

He spun quickly. He should leave. He knew he should, but he couldn't take one step toward the door. Suddenly, he heard a loud shriek and splash. He jerked back around in fright, dashing over to the pool. "Amelia!"

She surfaced and swiped at her wet hair. "I'm all right. I just tripped and fell back in."

"Let me help you." Michael held out his hand. Amelia took it, her other remaining clutched around her sodden bath towel. Michael assisted her out of the bathing pool, automatically putting an arm about her to steady her.

"Thank you," Amelia said, looking up at him.

"You're . . ." Michael murmured. She was warm, wet, and perfect in his arms. She was beautiful and his whole body cried out for her. He didn't finish his sentence, for there weren't any words he could speak . . .

—from "A Valentine from Venus," by Cindy Holbrook

WATCH FOR THESE ZEBRA REGENCIES

VALENTINE WISHES

Mona Gedney
Cindy Holbrook
Jeanne Savery

Zebra Books
Kensington Publishing Corp.

http://www.zebrabooks.com

Contents

Lady Diana's Courtship

Mona Gedney

"Of course I won't marry him," snapped Lady Diana. "How could you consider such an outrageous proposal? I don't even know him!"

"Come now, Di," pleaded her father. "There's no need to get into such a pelter over this. Be sensible and think of what a difference this marriage could make to us. At least meet the gentleman."

"Gentleman!" she returned bitterly, ignoring his plea. "He is no more a gentleman than you are a saint! Had you even a feather to fly with, you would never consider such an offer! Certainly you would never consider such a match for yourself."

Lady Diana, only daughter of the wastrel Earl of Glenwood, did not suffer fools gladly—and among that group she included her father, who had gambled away all of the family fortune that was neither entailed nor kept by his daughter under lock and key. His most recent losses had placed him in an extremely unpleasant position, for there were those who appeared to expect to receive the money owed them—even from a member of the peerage.

The earl sighed at the distressing injustice of life and turned his flawless countenance toward the fireplace, staring into the leaping flames as though they would provide an answer to his dilemma. He knew that neither his forlorn expression nor his classic good looks would win his daughter's sympathy. It really came as no surprise to him that Diana refused even to see John Derringer, the wealthy cit who had just offered for her.

After the earl had run himself all to pieces four years earlier, she had refused all of the wealthy men that he had selected for her, no matter how good their family or how charming their manner. Since she was a handsome girl of impeccable lineage herself, there had been no shortage of suitors, despite her family's desperate straits, but his daughter appeared to have no interest in any of them.

"I suppose he won my hand in one of the gaming hells you frequent!" she fumed.

"Of course he did not!" the earl exclaimed indignantly. "You have no right to accuse me of such dishonorable behavior, Diana!" And indeed he had not played with Diana's hand in marriage as the stake—even the earl knew his limits.

His daughter, still suspicious, was far from penitent. "You needn't think that I shall solve your problems for you by allowing you to sell me to the highest bidder, Father! I will be no sacrificial lamb to lay on the altar of your vices! I wouldn't do it even to save whatever of Tommy's inheritance there is left—and heaven knows that must be little enough!"

Her kindling eye caught his as he glanced up, and he looked quickly away, hoping that she would not guess the truth of the matter. Guilt was not an emotion that he allowed himself, tending instead simply to think in terms of what was necessary for his own comfort. However, if she would not marry for the sake of her brother Tommy, to whom she was devoted, then she certainly wouldn't consider doing so for any lesser reason—like the preservation of her father's health and sanity.

"Why, if I married this Derringer, you'd gamble away whatever he brought into the family before Tommy had a chance even to see it," she continued bitterly. "Then I'd be left with some beef-witted husband who wanted to marry into the *ton* so badly that he was willing to spend all of his hard-earned guineas on a peer that hasn't been sober in the past seven years! He would soon repent such a marriage, and I would pay the price!"

The earl sank into a chair and held his throbbing head in his hands. However he and his mild-mannered wife had brought the virago before him into the world was beyond his comprehension. His wife had gone to her grave in the same manner that she had lived her life: so unobtrusively that only her husband and children had been aware of her departure. No, Diana was a throwback, possibly to a far earlier time when the women of the family had led their people into battle—and probably eaten the hearts of their defeated enemy, he reflected bitterly.

Although he had not been optimistic about the outcome of John Derringer's offer, the earl had entertained the feeble hope that if she rejected the thought that she should do so to help her father—and he had been certain that she would reject it—she might at least sacrifice herself for the sake of her brother Tommy, the present Viscount Hartley, a happy-go-lucky young man who appeared cheerfully certain that all would turn out well for them, despite their father's ruinous course. Family loyalty was simply not what it once was, the earl reflected self-pityingly, his eyes drifting to a handsome painting of Meadowbrook, their primary residence in the country.

"Don't even think of trying to sell it!" said Diana sharply, following his gaze suspiciously. "That picture stays on the wall, and Meadowbrook itself is entailed, as you very well know. You cannot touch either of them."

The earl smiled beatifically—for her mention of Meadowbrook had inspired him. There might, after all, be a way around his headstrong daughter. He altered his smile to a suitably sad one and sighed deeply.

"I'm afraid that we must pack and take ourselves to Meadowbrook, my dear child. I am quite rolled up, you know, and keeping this house in town open takes more of the ready than I have just now. As you say, I would not have considered an offer such as Derringer's except that I am run quite off my legs. It is more than time to take a repairing lease in the country. You and Tommy can go down tomorrow, and I will follow directly."

Diana studied her father for a moment, searching for an ulterior motive, then nodded. "I shall tell Hannah to begin packing immediately," she agreed.

She was fearful that Tommy might follow in her father's footsteps, for he had been spending far too much time with some very fast friends. She had determined that she would not marry, even to please herself, as long as Tommy, who was several years her junior, needed her guidance. Certainly he would not receive it from his father.

And so it was that the earl managed to send his headstrong daughter and her brother to their country home, to which he had also invited John Derringer. Derringer might be a cit, the earl reflected craftily, but he had good blood in his background, and he was a tall, fine-looking man with pleasant ways. Once he got Diana to Meadowbrook, the earl would see to it that she could not get away for a while—at least long enough for Derringer to say his piece.

He had, after all, promised the man just such an opportu-

nity, and supplying it would at least satisfy one debt. And—
although he doubted it most seriously—there was always
the possibility that Diana might weaken when faced with
such an offer. The earl could not bear to see a fortune
like Derringer's move beyond his grasp. Why such a nota-
ble catch should be interested in Diana was a mystery to
him, for the sharpness of her tongue was legendary, but
he was not one to sneer in the face of Fortune. At the very
least, he would have another opportunity to sit down to
cards with a guest with well-lined pockets.

John Derringer, recently returned from several years
abroad in the army, had come to London to put his business affairs in order. He had been a rich man before leaving
England, but now, after the deaths of both his father and
uncle while he was away, his wealth bid fair to rival that
of the Golden Ball. He was keenly aware that this would
make him the target of countless young women and their
grasping parents, so he had been anxious to wind up his
affairs and get away to the country before they began to
stalk him. He had no social ambitions, and the thought
of what could lie ahead for him in London sped the transac-
tion of his business affairs considerably.

It was upon his third, and supposedly final, night in
London that he had attended the theatre. There he saw
Lady Diana Crosswell seated in a box across from him, and
discovered that love at first sight was not as far-fetched a
notion as he had thought it. Her beauty—the contrast of
pale skin with dark eyes and hair—caught his eye and held
it, as did the manner in which she held herself, and then
he heard her laughter as she turned to the gentleman
who had just whispered something in her ear. Despite her
obvious flirtation, there was nothing of the simpering miss

about her, he noted with approval, for her laughter was genuine and unaffected rather than coy.

Making it his business to discover her identity, he learned of her refusal to marry (like the Diana of Roman mythology, for whom she had been named) and of her father's desperate financial situation. He had waited upon that gentleman the next morning, introduced himself, and made the offer of marriage that Lady Diana had so promptly refused. Her father, distraught at the thought of Derringer's money slipping through his eager fingers, had been indiscreet enough to tell him her precise words in framing her tactless refusal.

"My apologies, Derringer," said the earl, shaking his head, "but those were her exact words to me—'He is no more a gentleman than you are a saint!' And, of course, I am no saint—but Diana is a little too high in the instep when she says that you are not a gentleman. She speaks from anger, not from any knowledge of you—and of course anyone who knows you would never call you beef-witted."

Derringer nodded his head grimly, thinking that he would like very much to point out to her that her words had scarcely been those of a lady. Irritated by her haughty attitude, that very night Derringer had played against the earl in an intimate little gaming hell with extremely high stakes, winning both the right to meet Diana and the right to court her. He had every intention of taking himself to Meadowbrook to teach the lady a much-needed lesson in good manners.

After his evening with Derringer, the earl was grateful that he had already announced to his children that he was closing the London house because of his finanacial affairs. Now there was absolutely no choice. He would have to do so. He shuddered as he thought of the possibility that Diana might discover the latest wagers he had lost to Derringer. Then, as he did with all unpleasant possibilities, he set it aside to be thought of no more.

"You're going *where?*" demanded Alexander Worth in disbelief, pausing midway in swallowing from his mug of breakfast ale to stare at his friend. The two had been dining for some ten minutes before Derringer had seen fit to share his news.

John Derringer calmly helped himself to another rasher of bacon, ignoring his friend's astonishment. A long friendship allowed Worth the freedom of frankness, even in the most personal matters. "You heard me well enough, Alex. I'm going to Meadowbrook as the guest of the Earl of Glenwood."

"Why?" asked Alex flatly. "What could you possibly have in common with him? He gambles and he loses and he drinks—and he gambles and he loses and then he drinks again. Is he having you there in the hope that he can fleece you?"

"Probably," nodded Derringer, unperturbed.

"I know he can't do it, of course," continued Worth, studying his friend. "You're too canny for that and you won from him the other night at Madame Renoir's—but he's badly dipped, you know, and he would take you if he could."

Derringer nodded again. "He would, indeed. But it isn't that which takes me there."

"Then what does? It can't be the charm of his company, for he's in his cups most of the time—and that pup of his is bidding fair to go the same way."

There was no reaction from Derringer as Worth chewed thoughtfully on a bite of beef, still staring at his friend. Suddenly he banged his fist on the table and grinned.

"Of course! It's the daughter, isn't it? The lovely—and deadly—Lady Diana."

Derringer did not betray himself by so much as the flicker of an eyelash, but his color deepened slightly, and Worth shook his head.

"Do you have any notion what you've let yourself in for, John?" Worth demanded. "You've been out of the country too long, or you'd never have given her more than a passing glance, no matter how handsome you think her. Why, she's turned down half the *ton*, quite as though she were the greatest prize in the marriage mart, which heaven knows she's not. Whoever marries her inherits all of Glenwood's debts and, to top off a bad bargain, gets a cold-hearted flirt who likes to call the tune."

He signaled to a footman to refill his tankard and raised it to his friend. "Take my advice, John, and don't go. There's nothing but trouble for you at Meadowbrook."

"Thank you for your concern, Alex," returned his friend calmly, folding his napkin and rising from the table, "but I assure you there's no reason to worry about me."

"You're going to go, aren't you?" sighed Worth. "Well, at least I've done the duty of a friend and told you that it's not the thing to do. I'd sooner see you taking up life as an Indian fakir lying on a bed of nails."

Derringer grinned. "I appreciate your good wishes, Alex. I shall expect you to dance at my wedding."

Worth shook his head dolefully. "Don't do it, John. You know all of the stories about the Roman goddess Diana from our school days, and you remember very well what happened to any young man who set his heart on her."

"Are you telling me, Alex, that the Lady Diana has vowed virginity and that she carries about her bow and arrows to strike down any man with the effrontery to woo her?"

Alex held out his open palms in a gesture of surrender. "There you have the truth of it, John. She will lead you on and then strike you down. If you're determined to fly in the face of fate by courting such a termagant, I might as well shoot you through the heart right now."

Derringer's laughter rang through the dining room. "You have always had a flair for the dramatic, Alex. I trust that my experience will be able to soften your view of the lady."

Still laughing, he walked briskly from the room, calling, "I'll see you in a few days, Alex."

His friend stared gloomily after him, shaking his head. "You'll never be the same, John," he murmured sadly into his tankard.

Diana was the first to arrive at Meadowbrook, and she and Hannah, their housekeeper, began setting the house to rights, having descended upon the staff with no warning. Tommy had invited a friend from school and was following them down in his curricle, and their father would join them later in the week.

It was always pleasant to come back here, Diana reflected, looking about the sunny drawing room with pleasure. Here at least little was changed. The pale yellow walls and the bright daffodil glow of the festooned draperies caught and reflected every gleam of winter sunshine. Everything about the room was cheerful and inviting, from the old-fashioned carved and gilt chimneypiece to the simple giltwood pier glasses. In the corner sat the japanned cabinet brought back from Italy by her grandfather some sixty years ago. The carpet was the same one she had known as a child, its rich colors of old gold and bittersweet faded but charming.

Meadowbrook still seemed like home, despite the fact that the earl had managed to strip away many of its treasures. Most of the valuable pieces brought home from abroad by her grandfather and great-grandfather had found their way into the private collections of those with whom the earl played cards. Even the occasional family portrait in the Long Gallery had been removed. This drawing room had been spared the earl's raids thus far, however, having been the private precinct first of his mother and then of his wife and daughter. Never anxious to confront Diana openly, he had wisely left intact the apartments most frequented by his family.

So it was that here she was able to feel at home in her surroundings, pausing to smile for a moment in front of the portrait of Tommy as a sweet-faced, slender boy of twelve. Her smile soon disappeared, however, replaced by a determined frown. Now a young man of twenty, Tommy's sweetness of nature appeared to be slipping away from him all too quickly. His recent weeks in London after leaving Oxford had been spent in the company of a fast group with a rather unsavory reputation, so Diana had welcomed her father's suggestion that they all retire to Meadowbrook. Since their relationship had always been close, she had every hope of separating him from the unwholesome influences to which he had been exposed.

Tommy had at first been reluctant to accept the idea, but he had finally been forced to realize that he had no choice.

"Well, I'll come if I must, Di," he had conceded, "but I'll be hanged if I'm coming without some decent company. I can't go into the country and live like a dashed hermit," he had told her.

"No one expects you to be a hermit, Tommy," she had replied briskly, "but you can't bring down one of those Captain Sharps you have been spending your time with."

He looked at her with an injured air. "Why would you think I'd do such a thing? Surely you can give me credit for *some* breeding—and what on earth would you know about Captain Sharps?"

She had ignored his query and, upon learning that his guest would be a Mr. Robert Wallace from his Oxford days, Diana had apologized gracefully, relieved that he would be out of harm's way for at least a few weeks.

When she strolled into the library at Meadowbrook late that afternoon, she was startled to find comfortably ensconced there a dark stranger, who stood and bowed to her.

"Good day, Lady Diana," he said, smiling down at her.

Thinking that he must be Tommy's friend, she returned his smile and extended her hand.

"Hello, Mr. Wallace," she said easily, pleased that she could remember the name that Tommy had given her. "I didn't realize that you and Tommy had arrived."

"Oh, I don't believe Tommy has arrived yet," returned the gentleman, "but he is doubtless on his way."

"Well, how shockingly unkind of him to send you on ahead, sir, when you don't know anyone," she returned gracefully.

"Ah, but I do now," he returned, his brown eyes warm. "And I am delighted to be here."

Lady Diana smiled at him, a genuine smile this time. Tommy's friends had never shown themselves to be as mannerly and personable as this very impressive gentleman. He was undoubtedly at least ten years Tommy's senior, and she wondered precisely how they had met at Oxford. He was, perhaps, a relative of one of Tommy's classmates—or perhaps, although it seemed unlikely—a tutor.

"It is chilly out, Mr. Wallace, but perhaps you would like to see the gardens," she commented, thinking that it would be a pleasure to show such a handsome and personable man the maze designed by her grandmother's grandmother. Even during the winter it was a delightful place to walk. "Since Tommy was so careless in his manners, you must allow me to make up for his oversight."

"I would be delighted," he responded, bowing. "I caught a glimpse of the maze from my window, but I didn't feel that I should make myself at home until I had made myself known to my hostess."

He smiled warmly. "Now that I have, I can think of nothing that I would rather do than walk with you, Lady Diana. If fortune smiles upon me, we shall become hopelessly lost."

Smiling and flirting—with due restraint—had become second nature to Diana, so she was highly pleased with his polished address and took his arm with pleasure, thinking that she must congratulate her brother upon his choice of a friend. Seldom had she had the pleasure of talking with one who was self-confident, handsome, *and* intelligent. All too often she had seen the first two qualities coupled, but seldom were they accompanied by intelligence. Although she did not plan to marry soon, she saw no reason not to indulge herself with a wide range of agreeable young men, and she was delighted to discover another possibility in Mr. Wallace.

The puzzle garden in which they strolled was an old one, designed some two hundred years earlier, its graceful intertwining loops the symbols of infinity.

"My great-great-grandmother designed this maze for lovers," remarked Lady Diana in what she hoped was a suitably casual voice. She had taken the arm of many a gentleman for just such a stroll, but she was curiously aware of the physical presence of the man walking beside her, far more than had been the case with any of the dozens of other young men who had paid court to her.

"Very charming," he replied, looking down into her

eyes rather than at the garden before them. "Puzzles have always fascinated me."

"Doubtless you would have enjoyed her then," said Lady Diana, meeting his glance demurely. "I am sorry that you must make do with me instead, sir."

He smiled appreciatively at this pleasantry and placed his gloved hand over hers, which rested lightly upon his arm, tucking it firmly into place and stirring an unfamiliar warmth within her. "I think that I shall manage nicely with you, Lady Diana," he responded, leading her into the maze.

"I begin to fear that you might." she murmured, suddenly finding it difficult to concentrate upon anything except his closeness. It was a heady feeling that she had not experienced before, and she knew instinctively that it was dangerous.

The walls of greenery shielded them from the wintry breeze and the view of any curious onlookers, providing the pair with a degree of intimacy that she found acutely disturbing. Diana had taken full advantage of this situation in the past, playing her suitors skillfully, like fish to be reeled in or cast away at will. Always she had felt herself to be entirely in control, even when the gentleman was too eager. Her coolness had always triumphed, damping the ardor of her companion at precisely the right moment. Now, however, disturbing though his closeness was, she did not want it ended. Even the slight pressure of his sleeve against her arm, of his hand upon hers, made her forget the chill of the winter afternoon. The current between them was so strong that she knew he too must be aware of it.

She gave herself a brief shake and forced herself to move away from him.

"Is there something wrong, Lady Diana?" he asked.

She shook her head. "No, nothing at all. I was suddenly aware of the cold—that's all."

To her distress, he put his arm around her shoulders protectively and turned her toward the entrance of the maze. "Then we must get you back to the house," he said briskly.

They left the maze and moved rapidly across the space between the garden and the side door to the house, Lady Diana doing her best to breathe evenly and to ignore his nearness. As he held open the door for her to enter, she saw that they were not alone.

"Tommy!" she exclaimed gratefully, glad of a distraction. "Your Mr. Wallace and I have half frozen to death walking in the garden. You should have been here to protect him from such a fate."

Her brother looked at them, puzzled, his smile fading. "My Mr. Wallace?" he asked doubtfully. "Di, *this* is Rob Wallace, the friend that I told you I was bringing down." And he indicated a fair-haired young man standing just behind him, who bowed and assured her that he was delighted to make her acquaintance.

Now as puzzled as her brother, Diana turned to the gentleman standing beside her. "And is your name Wallace, too, sir?" she asked.

He smiled and shook his head. "I'm afraid that I let you believe so, ma'am, but I assure you that I am quite legitimately a guest in your home—at the invitation of your father rather than your brother, however."

Diana's dark eyebrows drew closer together. "And your name, sir?" she asked in a brittle voice, certain of his response.

"John Derringer, ma'am, at your service," he responded, bowing, well aware that his very name would infuriate her.

"I should have suspected as much!" she snapped, a

gratifying rush of anger warming her. Gratefully she realized that it released her from the spell that he had laid upon her with his first touch. "I am certain that you will understand, Mr. Derringer, when I say that I no longer desire your company—and that I insist upon your leaving Meadowbrook immediately."

"Here now, Di!" exclaimed Tommy. "That's coming it too strong. Even if you're in a pelter with our father, you can't take it out on his guest! Damn it all, Di, he is our guest, too!"

Ignoring her brother's protests and young Mr. Wallace's wide-eyed bleats of distress (for he doubtless pictured the same thing happening to him), she turned and walked swiftly from the room, leaving the two young men to try to apologize to her victim.

"I daresay that she was affected by the cold," said young Mr. Wallace, struggling to look as though he believed it. "Young ladies are quite fragile, you know."

"No such thing! Di is an Amazon," responded her brother roughly. "She's simply taken it into her head to dislike you because you're a friend of our father," he explained to Derringer. "I won't say that she doesn't have some grounds for getting upset with the old man, but this is beyond reason, even for Di."

"I assure you, Lord Hartley, that I quite understand her distress—although I am not planning to leave at the moment," Derringer assured Tommy.

"You do?" asked Tommy blankly. "Damned if I do, and I'm her brother! Still, it's decent of you not to set your back up about her behavior. She'll come round, you know—or at least she usually does."

"Does she indeed?" inquired Derringer with interest. "What else has she 'come round' about?"

"Well, there was the time at Oxford that I had gotten in over my head—" he began.

"Owed more than you would receive for the next three quarter-days," observed Mr. Wallace knowledgeably. "Not a feather to fly with."

"And your sister was angry, but she finally helped you?" inquired Derringer, interested.

Both young gentlemen nodded vigorously. "Came through like a trouper," asserted Tommy. "She combed my hair for me properly, but she didn't leave me in the lurch—nor did she tell our father. Never has. She may fly off the handle, but she's loyal."

Derringer digested this information in interested silence. It appeared to cast Lady Diana in a more favorable light than he had seen her heretofore, for thus far he viewed her as a hardened flirt who set her own price far too high. He did not have long to reflect upon her character, however, for the two young gentlemen, determined to do their duty by him, bore him away to play billiards for the remainder of the afternoon.

It was after this that he mounted the stairs to his chamber to dress for dinner and encountered Lady Diana.

"I thought that I had asked you to leave this house, sir," she said coldly, avoiding his eyes.

"Well, you see, Lady Diana," he said apologetically, "since I am the earl's guest, I feel that I must, out of courtesy, await his arrival before leaving. I would appear most rag-mannered otherwise."

"And he won't arrive for two more days," she said bitterly. "Now I understand why he sent a note saying that his business affairs would keep him away for that long. He was hoping that I would no longer be angry when he arrived. Avoiding unpleasantness—especially if he is the cause of it—has been the business of his life."

She paused, still not directing her gaze at him, then

added, "I wonder at your remaining in a place where you are so clearly unwelcome, sir."

And, so saying, she turned and continued down the stairs.

"Do you indeed?" he inquired, directing his question to her back. "You surprise me, Lady Diana. I would have thought that you would expect exactly this behavior from one who is not a gentleman—and who is beef-witted, to boot."

Having delivered this home shot, he continued up the stairs to his chamber, not noting that she had frozen upon hearing his remark. So not even her conversations with her father were private, but were to be shared with total strangers like John Derringer, she reflected bitterly. For a fleeting moment she felt slightly guilty for her careless words, but the moment passed. If the man's sensibilities— had he any—had been wounded by the words she had spoken in private, she felt that she could scarcely be blamed for it. Her anger was directed toward her father for still another betrayal of confidence. Derringer would have to fend for himself.

As it happened, however, she had to fend for herself. Wherever she turned during the next day she seemed to encounter him. When she walked in the gardens in the morning, he appeared suddenly beside her, smiling and offering her his arm in such a manner that it was impossible to refuse him unless she turned and stepped directly into the reflection pond behind her in order to avoid him. When she went down for nuncheon, thinking that Tommy had borne him off riding and would stop at a nearby inn instead of returning home immediately, he was there, holding her chair for her to be seated and leaning over her far too closely for comfort. When she started up the stairway to her chamber later that afternoon, she encountered him coming down, and he stopped to ask how she had spent the afternoon and to admire her brooch, even though he was well aware that she wished to have no conversation with him at all.

Whenever she saw him, Mr. Derringer seemed to take full advantage of the opportunity to stand closer to her than propriety dictated. Refusing to pull away as though she were intimidated, which she suspected was precisely what he wanted, Diana maintained her poise each time and acted as though his proximity were perfectly natural and disturbed her not at all. In truth, however, it disturbed her far more than she could admit to herself.

The final encounter before dinner that evening occurred in the library. Derringer knew of course the reason for her cool treatment of him, and he was certain of the effect his presence was having upon her. He was quite determined to shake her from her distant politeness, the shield behind which she was hiding herself, and to force a genuine reaction from her. When he found her in the library, he began amusing himself by making observations to her that he knew would rankle. At first his ploy met with little success as he made comments about her flirtations and about her reputation for heartlessness and drew no reaction at all, but then he began to muse over her name.

"You know, Lady Diana, your father said that your mother chose your name. I believe he said that she loved Roman mythology." He drew deeply upon the cigar that he had just lighted and studied her profile as she sat with her book, doing her best to ignore him.

"I can see that sort of cool, dark beauty that she was noted for—Diana being the goddess of the moon and all that, you know." He mused a moment, staring reflectively at the glowing ash of his cigar; then he laughed. "And he said—"

Here he stopped abruptly and looked at her apologetically. "I'm sorry, ma'am. From time to time I forget that I am in a lady's company. I've been too much with men, I'm afraid."

Silence fell for several minutes until Diana closed her book with a snap. "Go ahead and tell me, sir. Just what did my father have to say? That it was improper I have no doubt!"

"Oh, I don't think it would be the thing for me to tell you, Lady Diana," he demurred, delighted that his ruse had worked. She had at least really spoken to him, instead of dismissing him with distant, disinterested remarks.

"You showed no delicacy about your proposal to me, Mr. Derringer. I must insist, sir, that you tell me what my father has been saying!"

"I'm afraid that the earl blames your name for your propensity to dislike men and to refuse to marry. Diana, as he reminded me, was the goddess of virgins and young unmarried women," he explained apologetically, tactfully refraining from looking at her.

"Precisely what I might expect of him!" she said bitterly. "And he was saying all of this to strangers in some smoke-filled hell while he gambled away what little money we have left!" She looked disdainfully at his cigar, which he hurriedly dropped into the fire, and then glared at him. "And I suppose that you laughed at his comment and encouraged him!"

Derringer shook his head. "I told him that I would like very much to meet someone named for a goddess." He hesitated a moment, then madness overtook him and he added, "We played for my right to meet you—and I won." Such a comment was not typical of him, for he had always been courteous and respectful in his treatment of women, regardless of their behavior toward him.

Diana slapped him smartly, then turned her back, her shoulders stiff. Nothing was said for a moment, then she spoke quietly. "I beg your pardon, Mr. Derringer. It is my father who is at fault. He indeed should have known better."

"And I, being the poor cit I am, having no breeding, cannot be expected to act the part of a gentleman?" he inquired dryly, remembering her comments about him and his offer.

"Can you say that what you did was the act of a gentleman, Mr. Derringer?" she demanded, her eyes bright with anger. "Was it the way you would wish for your sister or your daughter to be treated?"

Derringer looked down at her, his eagerness to punish her fading. He thought of the earl's behavior and of her attempts to help her brother and to keep their family together and was suddenly ashamed of the way he had reacted in anger—something he had never been guilty of before.

"No, it was not," he returned soberly, "and you have my apology and my word—as a former officer, if not in your eyes a gentleman—that I will never be guilty of such an act again."

He had no wish to pain her by adding that he had attempted that night to quiet the earl's rather raucous remarks about his daughter. Diana had recently refused two offers that her father considered very worthy ones, and his bitterness that evening had been great, amplified by the brandy he had been drinking.

Derringer walked to the door, closing it quietly behind him. He no longer felt that he belonged here. All desire to punish the young lady had faded, and now he was a man without a mission in a lonely outpost.

To Tommy's disgust, Diana refused to dine with the gentlemen that evening, informing him that she had no intention of spending any more time than she could avoid in the company of such a man as Derringer. Not being aware of the proposals or its aftermath, he had viewed her refusal as simple snobbery.

"But he's a great gun, Di!" he told her seriously. "Why, he's served with Wellington, although we can't get him to talk too much about the fighting yet. And you should see the pair that he drove down here! I've never seen a finer set-out of blood and bone. Why are you on your high ropes, Di? Is it because he's a cit?"

"It really doesn't matter, Tommy," she responded shortly. "You and Mr. Wallace may enjoy his company with my blessing—only I trust that he'll be gone tomorrow instead of waiting for our father's arrival."

"Gone tomorrow!" exclaimed her brother indignantly. "I should say that he won't! Why, Rob and I have only just convinced him to take us out and show us how to take my curricle around a corner without breaking pace or oversetting it. Derringer's a top-sawyer!"

"I suppose he told you so himself," Diana remarked dryly, more than a little nettled by his defense of the man who had so recently been a stranger.

"Indeed he didn't—wouldn't, you know. Not his sort of remark. Rob saw him in town when he stopped a runaway carriage coming around a busy corner by pulling up alongside it without oversetting it or his own curricle or running over anyone. Rob said there was applause from the crowd on the street, but Derringer just checked on the old gentleman in the carriage, then went on his way, ignoring it all."

"Did he indeed?" she asked in a bored tone, though she was caught by the story. "I suppose you asked him about that, too, and he told you all about it."

"Dash it all, Di, don't you listen to anything I tell you?" demanded Tommy. "Naturally he wouldn't do such a thing. He's a gentleman even though he's a cit. He pokered up when Rob told the story, and we couldn't get anything out of him."

"Nonetheless," replied his sister, "I'm not interested in hearing any more stories about Mr. Derringer. I can only hope that we are relieved of his presence soon. As you so crudely observed, he *is* a cit. He's not one of us."

Tommy looked at her incredulously, then said slowly, "You're right about that, of course, Di. He's *not* one of us. His manners wouldn't allow him to treat a chambermaid the way you're treating him. I daresay he wonders what he's doing among such a set of boors."

Stung by his unaccustomed criticism—and more than a little uneasy at the thought that he might be right—Diana adjourned to her chamber to dine in solitary splendor and meditate over her brother's remarks. He was merely impressed by Derringer's army experience and his apparent prowess with horses, of course. Boys could be expected to be overwhelmed by such things, but she was not to be taken in so easily. Particularly by one who had gained her confidence—and the favor of her company—under false pretenses. Tommy simply did not understand the whole situation. She had only to remember his offer—which had not been made in person—and the manner in which he had gambled to win the right to come to their home in order to fire her temper again.

Nonetheless, still smarting from Tommy's unjust comparison of her behavior with that of Derringer, the next morning she went down to breakfast determined to demonstrate that she, too, could be gracious. It was therefore a disappointment to discover that Mr. Derringer had already dined and gone out for his morning ride, joined by the admiring Tommy and Rob. Having no one to whom she could demonstrate her graciousness had a decidedly foul effect upon her humor, and she ate her breakfast with an injured air.

Her resolution to smile coolly and nod distantly whenever Mr. Derringer spoke to her was put to the test only an hour or two later. Diana was in the Long Gallery, carefully checking the catalog she had made of its contents and noting with irritation that the earl had once again removed a valuable portrait, despite his promise that nothing more would be removed from Meadowbrook.

It was at this inauspicious moment that John Derringer appeared, still dressed in his riding gear. Although his buckskin breeches and jacket of blue superfine fit him to perfection, proclaiming his patronage of no less a tailor than Weston, Diana could not view him with admiration. Forgotten was the brief but intense attraction that she had felt for him two days before, for he was at a safe distance. What she saw was another of her father's gambling associates, one who wished to rob her not only of the possessions that belonged to the family, but of her very freedom.

"Good morning, Lady Diana," he said, drawing closer. "I apologize for interrupting you." Here he gestured to the catalog that she carried. "Actually, I've come to apologize for my intrusion upon your family circle, and to take my leave of you."

Diana had been fully prepared to give him the benefit of her pent-up anger, but his final remark slowed her, and then she saw Tommy appear suddenly in the doorway behind Derringer.

"Take your leave?" Tommy exclaimed. "But you can't do that! You've only just begun to show Rob and me how to drive."

He stopped to stare at his sister. "Have you been after him again, Di?" he demanded.

Derringer raised his hand before she could reply. "No, she has not—although I know that I have intruded upon her privacy and it would be her right to 'take after me' again."

"Nonsense—" began Tommy, but he was interrupted by his sister.

"Tommy is quite right," she said quickly, ignoring Derringer's surprise. She had been surprised in turn by his defense of her, but more pressing than that, she was quite sure that the earl would not come down to Meadowbrook if she allowed Derringer to leave—and she very badly wished to confront him with his most recent depredations there. "Your leaving is nonsense, Mr. Derringer. You must wait for our father, and we will hope that you will survive the tender attentions of my brother and Mr. Wallace."

Derringer's eyes brightened at this unexpected respite. "Are you sincere, ma'am? I have your invitation to stay?"

Diana swallowed, but she managed to maintain a calm expression. His brown eyes were uncomfortably warm, and she grew restive under his steady gaze, but she kept her voice cool and steady. "Yes, of course you do, sir. We should be glad to have your company. I can see that you will be kept desperately busy."

Derringer ignored Tommy's cheerful invitation to come downstairs with him directly so that they could resume their driving lessons, walking instead toward her with his hand extended.

"How kind you are, Lady Diana," he murmured, leaning over her hand, "to overlook my careless behavior and invite me to remain."

Diana nodded briefly, trying to maintain the fiction that having her hand held in his was not a noteworthy event. Once again she was far too sharply aware of his nearness, and she made a mental resolution to keep a safe distance from him at all future times. Making a feeble excuse, she left his presence as soon as possible.

Derringer was left to meditate upon the problem of his courtship in the company of Tommy and Rob Wallace, who were fully determined to learn from him how to do things "bang up to the nines." When they discovered that he was no longer with Diana, they bore him away with them so that he could show them his prowess with a gun, and they could attempt to impress him with their own.

Diana, watching from the library window as they departed, allowed herself to be consoled by the steadying influence he appeared to have on Tommy. At least John Derringer was far better than the crowd Tommy had spent his time with in London—and, as a matter of fact, a far better influence than his own father. She would have to be grateful for that and endure Mr. Derringer's presence for the moment.

Her resolution to keep a safe distance from him, however, proved impossible to keep. Indeed, she soon no longer really attempted to do so, for she discovered that she enjoyed his easy conversation and his humor. To her surprise, she found him remarkably well read and began ruefully to amend her former view of him.

"Tell me, Diana, Lady of the Night, is that your favorite time?" he inquired the next afternoon, or are you a person who loves only the sunshine?"

"I love them both," she informed him. "However, I believe that I do favor the night."

"Of course you do," called her brother, who had strolled into the room in time to hear her final comment. "That is when you carry on the majority of your flirtations, Di. Without the night you would have far fewer scalps than you have now."

Diana flushed delicately. "He is just down from Oxford, you know," she said lightly. "We are trying to reinstill some manners, but I fear it will take some time."

Before Derringer could respond, Tommy had stuck his head back in the door, and called, "There's no hope for you, sir. She favors blue eyes, you know." He winked at his sister, who glared at him, and once again disappeared from sight.

"Well, that is a grave matter," said Derringer seriously. "I shall have to see what can be done about it."

Diana looked at him uncertainly. "About Tommy's manners, do you mean?" she asked.

He shook his head, his brown eyes meeting hers. "About changing the color of my eyes," he noted unsmilingly. "If you favor blue, something will have to be done." Very deliberately he had not turned his gaze from hers, and she began to feel like a rabbit being charmed by a cobra—quite as vulnerable—and it was a most unaccustomed emotion.

Normally she would have replied that she found his eyes delightful and that he must upon no account change anything about himself, but she could not bring herself to indulge in the old familiar dialogue, used so often with so many of her flirts. She managed to laugh lightly and to change the subject, but she was not deceived. Derringer was a man she would have to be very careful about.

By the time the earl arrived two days later, however, she had slipped into a comfortable and much more friendly relationship with their guest, going so far as to have two or three private conversations with him. He very carefully did not make her nervous in any way, playing the part of an older brother, free of any hint of flirtation.

When her father finally put in an appearance, Diana forced herself to speak to Derringer about the earl's gambling habits.

"He does gamble compulsively, you know," she said honestly, "and he will win from you anything that he can, so you must be on your guard. In fact, it would be best not to play with him."

To her disappointment, however, Derringer played cards with him, allowing the earl to win frequently, despite her disapproval. There had been no card games until the earl arrived, Derringer and the two younger gentlemen

being perfectly satisfied with billiards. Greatly to their cha-
grin, Tommy and Rob were not allowed to sit down to
cards with the two older gentlemen, Derringer telling them
unfeelingly that the stakes were too high for them, the
earl forbidding it because he knew that Tommy would lose
and he had no wish to become responsible for his son's
gambling debts. His own were quite enough.

Derringer and the earl were still sitting at their game
late one frosty night as Diana was making her evening
rounds before retiring to be certain that the servants had
secured all of the windows and doors. It was a duty that
the earl had never thought of performing and that Diana
had taken upon herself for many years.

The door to the earl's study stood open, throwing a
rectangle of glowing light upon the polished wood walls
of the corridor. Diana walked softly toward it, holding her
guttering candle carefully, until she heard the comfortable
sound of familiar voices. She did not intend to eavesdrop
but merely to determine that all was well—until she heard
her own name mentioned. Caught, she paused and listened.

"I saw you talking with my daughter this afternoon,"
the earl remarked. "Are you making any headway with
her?"

She stiffened in the silence. There was a long pause,
and then Derringer remarked in so quiet a voice that she
had difficulty making out his words. "We were merely
talking about the hunter that Tommy just purchased and
whether or not he was worth the price."

The earl snorted. "The boy knows that he shouldn't be
sporting his blunt on fripperies such as that. He's not to
be trusted to keep his spending within bounds."

Diana would have loved nothing so much as bursting
into the room to confront her father with his own excesses,

but she restrained herself and was pleased to hear that there was no necessity for her to do so.

"I believe, sir, if you will forgive my saying so," said Derringer, measuring his words, "that he is doing no more than modeling himself after his father—which is said to be the ultimate compliment, you know."

The earl was not to be put off by the supposedly complimentary afterthought that Derringer attached to his criticism. "That's as good as saying I go about throwing away my money with both hands! That's a pretty thing to say to your host, Derringer!" he remarked sharply. "I would think that you would remember whose guest you are."

"I am not forgetting, sir—nor am I forgetting that I won the right to be here. I know, however, that you should be very concerned about your son. He tells me that he will come into quite a pretty amount when he comes of age in a month. He will need a guiding hand if he is to keep his head then, and not throw away his fortune hand over fist."

"I shall see to that," the earl assured him.

"If you mean that, Lord Glenwood, that you have plans for the money yourself, I believe you underestimate your son. He has every intention of controlling the money himself."

There was a sudden sharp sound, as though the earl were throwing back his chair from the table, and then Diana could hear the sound of him pacing the room.

"You would think that I could have at least one grateful child—but no! I must be cursed with two of the most ungrateful whelps in all of Christendom!" exclaimed the earl bitterly. "They never give a thought to their father or what is necessary for my comfort!"

"I believe that your daughter has given a great deal of time and attention to her brother, however, and to what is necessary for his well-being," remarked Derringer calmly. "I should be very grateful if I had one child so willing to help another."

"That's easy enough for you to say, sir. You are not inconvenienced by her—and you *are* infatuated by her—though I could never imagine why! She has had enough offers to free me from my debts many times over, but she refuses to accept any of them! She is as heartless a wench as any I have ever known!"

Derringer's voice was cold as he replied. "I would thank you, Lord Glenwood, to remember that you are speaking of a lady who is your daughter—and that she scarcely need sell herself for your convenience."

"You needn't get so stiff-rumped about it," returned the earl querulously. "I may have been two sheets to the wind at the time, but I remember very well how high-handed you got at White's when I complained about my own child. There's no need to take that tone with me again."

"You may have been complaining about your own child, but the Lady Diana is not to be talked about in clubs in the manner in which you were doing it—and so I pointed out to you. I am grateful you remember so that I need not make my point again."

"Very well, very well," conceded Glenwood. "It was good of you not to tell her about the things I said that night. God knows I would rather talk about anything other than her ingratitude! Deal the cards, Derringer."

The only sound for the next few minutes was the soft shuffling and dealing of the cards and the clinking of crystal decanter against crystal glass, and Diana turned and tiptoed softly back down the corridor. Her father's behavior was precisely what she would have expected of him, but Derringer's was much more gentlemanly than she would at first have expected it to be. In fact, she thought, he put the earl to shame. Clearly birth did not automatically make one a gentleman in manner and thinking.

So it was that Diana went down to breakfast the next morning in brighter spirits than she had for some time. She had always known what to expect of her father, so his behavior came as no revelation. Their guest's behavior, however, had completely disarmed her, for she had never before had a defender. She was prepared to view John Derringer with a far more favorable eye than she had thus far. In fact, if things stood otherwise with her family situation, she might consider his suit—at least briefly.

"Good morning, Mr. Derringer," she said cheerfully as she took her place at the table. "I am surprised to see that you are up so early. You must have gotten little rest, for you and my father were still playing cards when I went to bed last night."

"I require very little rest, Lady Diana," he replied pleasantly, "but it is kind of you to be concerned about my welfare."

"Of course he needs little, Di," said Tommy, who had just entered the room with Rob. "In the field one has to be ready at the drop of a hat—awake and alert in a moment. Isn't that so, sir?" he added, appealing to Derringer.

His idol nodded in amusement. "When your life may hang in the balance, you tend to be a little brisker and quicker than you might under ordinary circumstances."

"See, Di. What did I tell you? He always turns everything that he does into a joke—as though it didn't count for much of anything when anyone with half an eye can see that it does."

Diana nodded, looking at John Derringer. "Yes, Tommy,

I begin to see that you may well be in the right of it in your assessment of Mr. Derringer."

Tommy glowed at this unexpected concession. "I knew that you would come to see the truth of it, Di! He is a right one."

Rob murmured his agreement as he applied himself to his breakfast, and John Derringer merely smiled absently in acknowledgment of their praise. If he was surprised by her mark of approval, he hid it well, moving the conversation immediately to other, more impersonal ground so that he wouldn't frighten her away.

"Although it's cold, it is a sunny morning. Perhaps you will ride with us today, Lady Diana," he said, ignoring the downcast expressions of Tommy and Rob, who had hoped to monopolize his time in their attempts to take the fences as he did.

"Thank you, Mr. Derringer. I believe that I will," she said, smiling at him—smiling directly into his eyes this time, instead of coolly over his head, as though he did not really exist.

To the ill-concealed disappointment of his two followers, the morning ride with Diana immediately became a habit. The two young men, hopeful that they would be able to steal him away, stuck close to Derringer and Diana on the first morning or two, but seeing that they had no hope of winning him away from the lady, soon gave up riding with them altogether. Nor was Derringer disappointed by their absence. And, if the truth were told, Diana did not miss them either. She and Derringer had become so involved in their own conversations that they had little time to spare for someone else.

"It's really rather shabby of you, Di," complained Tommy, as she arrived home after their fifth morning ride alone.

"What is?" she inquired absently, as she started up the stairs to her chamber to change.

"Stealing Derringer away in such a low female fashion," he returned. "Rob and I can't compete against you. It's really too bad that you've set him up as one of your flirts."

"I haven't!" said Diana quickly. "It's nothing of the sort."

"You know very well that it is. I've watched you with too many others not too know your pattern. You're being sweet as sugar to him now, encouraging him in every way possible, and then—just when he thinks that perhaps you really are interested—you'll lower the axe and send him packing."

"I'll do no such thing!" she said sharply.

"To be sure you will," returned Tommy bitterly. "I've seen it with Ashton, and Sir Jason, and Loveless—you know that I could list names from now until I go to bed tonight. You make eyes at them and lead them on, and then you turn cold as ice and send them on their way as though nothing at all had happened."

"Do you really think that I am capable of treating Mr. Derringer so unjustly?" she demanded. "I would never consider doing such a thing!"

"You see, Tommy, I told you," said Rob in a timid voice. "Didn't seem to me that Lady Diana was capable of such a mean trick."

"That's because you haven't seen her at work," said Tommy. "After she dropped him, Will Loveless told me that the men all talk about her 'Won't you step into my parlor?' eyes. The look invites them, and then, when they take the invitation, it's all over."

"You know that Will Loveless is merely angry because I didn't accept him," replied Diana. "You're really much too sensitive, Tommy."

"I told him that very thing," inserted Rob earnestly.

"You can't be thinking that about Lady Diana I told him. She—"

"Stuff and nonsense, Rob!" interrupted his friend rudely. "You know very well that you're half in love with her yourself. You've fallen for that look, just like all the others!"

Rob blushed to the roots of his fair hair, but he held his ground. "That's not the way to talk about your sister, Tommy," he insisted gallantly. Turning to Diana, he added, "We miss having Mr. Derringer's company, and I think that's the root of the problem."

Diana smiled at him gratefully, causing his blush to intensify to a deep scarlet. "Thank you, Rob," she said, kissing him gently on the cheek before she left the room.

"Oh, for pity's sake, Rob! She's far too old for you!" she heard Tommy saying as she closed the door behind her. "You have certainly made a cake of yourself!"

John Derringer, who had entered the house quietly through another door, had listened to the exchange with a smile. After the participants had gone their various ways, he took the stairway to his chamber to change from his riding gear. Things were looking better than he had dared to hope, and he looked forward to the rest of the day with anticipation. He had waited patiently for an opportunity to present his suit again, and the time appeared to be growing ripe. He had thought that he would wait until Valentine's morning, some three days away, to propose to Diana. It appeared, however, that he might be able to do so earlier.

The peacefulness of their situation was about to be disturbed, however. As he returned to the main hall of Meadowbrook after changing, he could hear the clatter that announced a new arrival. In the midst of the furor caused by Rob and Tommy and several of the hunting dogs that had followed them in from the court stood a tall, slender man, immaculately outfitted in black.

As Derringer entered, the man turned and lifted one dark eyebrow inquiringly at Tommy. The young man turned to see his friend and flushed.

"Oh, that's right. The two of you don't know each other, although that doesn't seem possible. Sir Jason, this is John Derringer. Mr. Derringer, Sir Jason Crume."

The two men bowed briefly to one another, inspecting one another with much the same wariness as dogs do when attack may be imminent. Derringer had not met Sir Jason, although he knew him by reputation—and the reputation was nothing to his credit. Sir Jason, on the other hand, knew virtually nothing of Derringer, except for the fact that he was tall and well made and appeared to handle himself like one of those who boxed with Gentleman Jackson.

Tommy turned to Derringer, his eyes bright. "How famous that both of you will be here together! I hadn't thought to have such luck!"

"Yes, I feel fortunate indeed," observed Sir Jason in a lazy voice that indicated quite the opposite. Turning to Tommy, he inquired, "Where is your lovely sister, Hartley?"

"She'll be along soon," he replied. "Di and Mr. Derringer were planning to go for a walk. It's all Rob and I can do to steal him away from her for an hour or so."

"Is that so?" asked Sir Jason, his voice sharpening a little at this news. He turned to assess Derringer more closely. "I suppose you have been warned about Lady Diana," he said lightly.

Derringer looked at him. "And why would that be necessary, Sir Jason?"

"Why, because she is the most heartless flirt between

here and Paris," he responded. "It would be difficult to estimate the number of hearts she has broken."

"Including yours," said Rob observantly, earning himself a dark look from Sir Jason and a chuckle from Derringer.

"Then I understand your warning, Sir Jason, and I shall do my best not to follow your lead."

Sir Jason, displeased with the turn of the conversation, gave his attention to Tommy and Rob, telling them about his latest gambling escapade the night before in an exclusive little hell in Mayfair.

"Everything depended on my final card," he told them casually. "I could have won or lost ten thousand pounds. As it happened, I won."

"Of course you did!" exclaimed Tommy admiringly. "Who can equal you at the gaming tables, Sir Jason? You have a cooler head than any of us."

Rob, who had not forgotten their days spent with Derringer, added, "You'll like Mr. Derringer, Sir Jason. Why, he has had to be cool even in the face of death. He was a major under Wellington."

"Indeed?" asked Sir Jason, surveying the other man with disfavor. "How very impressive."

"And I, sir, am equally impressed," returned Derringer dryly.

At this auspicious moment, Diana entered the hall, dressed for their walk in a green woolen pelisse.

"Ah, Lady Diana, what a pleasure it is to see you!" exclaimed Sir Jason, coming forward to bow and to seize her hand.

"Sir Jason!" she exclaimed, her tone indicating anything but pleasure as she turned to gaze reproachfully at her brother. "I had no idea that we were expecting you."

"Hartley mentioned to me that you would be here through the end of the month, and I thought that I would stop by on my way north to spend some time with my brother. After all," he added, lifting her hand to his lips with a meaningful look, "how could I be apart from you on Valentine's Day, dear lady?"

"How indeed?" she responded dryly, reclaiming her hand. "If you will excuse us, Mr. Derringer and I were just going out. I'm afraid that I must leave you to Tommy's tender mercies."

Her tone of voice betrayed no such fear, however, and she ignored his darkling gaze as they turned to walk to the door.

"They appear quite cozy," he remarked to Tommy as the door closed behind them.

Tommy grinned. "It would be all right with me if Derringer finally melted that icy heart of hers. Things appear to be moving in that direction."

Rob nodded knowledgeably. "The two of them go about smelling of April and May," he said sagely. "It's just a matter of time."

Sir Jason appeared disagreeably impressed with this news, and the two young men remembered uncomfortably that the gentleman might still be laboring under the strain of a broken heart.

Hurriedly, Tommy said, "Now that you're here, Sir Jason, we shall have a real evening of gambling. Derringer will play with no one save my father, and Rob and I have grown very tired of playing billiards in the evening. We sneak out now and then for an evening at the Golden Rule, but there's nothing there to equal the play that you can offer."

"How very true," agreed that gentleman. "We shall begin this very evening after dinner."

Tommy thought uneasily of what his sister's view of this was likely to be. "Perhaps, Sir Jason, it might be as well to wait until later in the evening," he suggested.

Rob, who had followed his thinking with no problem, added helpfully, "After Lady Diana has retired."

"I see," replied Sir Jason. "Very wise. Very wise indeed, gentlemen. I congratulate you upon your finesse."

The two young men smiled, feeling themselves to be very devious indeed. "Awake on every suit," agreed Rob happily.

"I'm sorry that Sir Jason has come," said Diana as they entered the garden, the brisk wind whipping the pink into her cheeks.

"If you're apologizing to me, there is no need, Lady Diana," Derringer responded. "But if, as I expect, you are sorry that he is here in company with your brother and young Wallace, I must agree. Has he really come because of Valentine's Day?"

She smiled ruefully. "Hardly that. Sir Jason knows that I have no wish to give him even the briefest of nods when we meet. He is, I am certain, after Tommy. He comes into his fortune next month, you know—or at least it seems a fortune to us. I daresay that to you it is the merest pin money."

Derringer ignored the reference to his wealth and pursued the subject that interested him most. "You're not interested in Sir Jason, then?" he inquired.

Diana shook her head emphatically. "Only insofar as he affects Tommy," she replied. "And I fear that he plans to coax Tommy into gambling with him—not that it would require much coaxing. And Tommy has no head for cards, even though he thinks himself so awake upon every suit."

Derringer nodded. "I would have expected as much," he agreed. "From what little I have heard of the man, he preys upon striplings like Tommy. He would rob your brother of everything if he had the opportunity."

"Well, at least Tommy has none of his money as yet," observed Diana.

"That certainly won't stop a man like Sir Jason," said Derringer. "He will simply take his vouchers and collect them in as soon as Tommy comes of age."

Diana grew pale as she thought this over and realized the truth of it. "Then we must stop him!" she said, agitated.

"We will," Derringer assured her calmly. "You may safely leave it to me, ma'am."

Strangely enough, even though she had known Derringer only a few days, Diana felt that she could unhesitatingly entrust him with her brother's welfare. "Thank you," she said gratefully, her eyes warm as she looked up at him.

She realized a moment later that she had leaned toward him as she looked up to him, for the invitation was too much for Derringer to resist. There in the privacy of the maze, he wrapped her in his arms and happily accepted her thanks.

Although the month was February and the air was sharp, neither Diana nor Derringer was in the least aware of it. His lips were warm against hers, and none of her flirtations had prepared her for the intensity of her response. All notions of propriety fled, and she gave herself to the joy of the moment. Just how long they remained there was uncertain, for the cold had no effect on them and the month could just as easily have been May so far as they were concerned.

"And do you not feel the cold, sir?" she murmured at last, regaining her breath.

"Not when I'm with you," he replied softly, his breath warm against her skin.

"And do you still wish to marry me, John Derringer?" she asked, turning to look full into his eyes.

He studied her for a moment as though thinking it over, but gave it up when she drew his lips down to hers again.

"Should we make it a Valentine's Day wedding?" he inquired at last.

"So soon?" she asked, startled.

He shrugged, his eyes dancing. "Why not? If you are going to marry a beef-witted cit, shouldn't you begin rehabilitating me as soon as possible? Perhaps with a little luck you can make me presentable by Christmas."

Diana responded to this sally as it deserved, and it was some time before the pair emerged from the maze.

Dinner that evening was far from enjoyable for anyone concerned. Diana and Derringer, fearful of revealing too much, tried to avoid one another's eyes. Her manner was cool and his was aloof as they longed for the meal to end. The earl was clearly irritated by the presence of a sharpster who would naturally wish to play cards during his visit; the earl wished to fleece Derringer himself and he certainly did not wish for Sir Jason to encroach upon Tommy's fortune, for which he still had his own plans. Sir Jason, who had planned a little elegant dalliance with Diana, was put out by her obvious fascination with the low-bred stranger, and, accustomed as he was to having the undivided admiration of Tommy and Rob, he was annoyed to see that they also admired the upstart newcomer. The young men themselves were uncertain about what their behavior should be so that they would upset neither Sir Jason or Derringer. Rob, who had military aspirations, was disposed to give the palm to Derringer, but Tommy, who appeared to have gaming in his blood, seemed to be fatally attracted to Sir Jason for the sake of sitting down to a serious game of cards.

Lady Diana withdrew immediately after dinner, announcing that she was retiring to her chamber but that coffee would be served in the library. Glancing at Derringer, she smiled and nodded, her gaze passing above Sir Jason and her father. Irritated, Sir Jason promised himself that the minx would pay for her slight.

"Well, gentlemen, now that we are alone, shall we sit down to a friendly game?" he inquired jovially, glancing about the table.

Tommy and Rob rose eagerly, having awaited this moment since Sir Jason's arrival. The earl was less eager, but he could think of no graceful way to avoid the game. Derringer simply smiled as he rose from the table and led the way to the library. The others followed him, Sir Jason annoyed by being upstaged and the earl trailing after everyone else, trying to determine his strategy for the evening.

As they arranged themselves comfortably about the table in the library, Sir Jason withdrew a deck of cards from his jacket and began to shuffle them.

The earl watched him with irritation. The upstart was planning to take things out of his hands in Meadowbrook, his own home! Smiling wickedly, he took out his own deck.

"No need to trouble yourself, Sir Jason," he remarked, shuffling his with a graceful flick of the wrist.

"No trouble at all, Glenwood," he returned. "Happy to be of service."

"Quite determined, aren't you?" inquired the earl. "Fuzzed the cards, have you?"

Tommy and Rob stared at him in horror, expecting Sir Jason to demand satisfaction of him immediately and retire to the garden with a pair of dueling pistols.

No such thing occurred. The earl and Sir Jason stared at each other for a moment, then Sir Jason said carefully, still shuffling, "I would imagine that you know more about that than I would."

There was another gasp from the two young men, then Derringer laid out a new deck in the middle of the table. "Let's call it a draw, gentlemen," he suggested gently.

"This deck hasn't yet been opened. Lord Glenwood, why don't you open it and inspect it, then pass it to Sir Jason? If it passes your inspection, we will use it."

Both men examined it closely and pronounced it acceptable, eyeing one another uneasily all the while.

"It looks good enough," said Sir Jason reluctantly. "Let's have Lord Hartley deal."

The others nodded their agreement, and Tommy began to deal the cards. The play proceeded quietly enough for an hour or two, all of them giving their attention to the game.

Derringer won steadily, and finally Tommy said with a reproachful laugh, "You know, it's really too bad of you to win our blunt, Derringer, when you already have more than enough to pave London in gold."

Sir Jason looked up sharply at this, for Derringer's financial status was news to him—although certainly happy news. Rob caught his glance and nodded happily, glad to be able to share information. "Rich as Croesus," he announced. "Maybe richer," he added thoughtfully.

"No need to shout it from the rooftops," said the earl in annoyance. "The rest of us may not be that wealthy, but we do have money that we're not easily parted from."

That statement was all too true, reflected Sir Jason unhappily. He had expected to be doing far better than he presently was, and now that he knew that he had a potential pigeon that was worth his weight in gold, he was unhappier still. Finally, though, his luck began to turn, and the earl lost to him steadily. Tommy, however, remained out of his grasp, playing with careful determination and managing to break even. Rob had put his head down on his hands and was openly sleeping, having already lost his quarter's allowance. Derringer had won as much as Sir Jason himself—and had in fact won most of his stack from Sir Jason, which was a tender point with that gentleman.

After another hour the earl sighed and threw down his cards. "I shall have to call it a night," he murmured. "I fear that I am out of cash."

"No need to let that trouble you," said Sir Jason. "Your voucher would always be acceptable, Glenwood—or perhaps we should make the stakes more interesting still."

The earl looked at him, his interest won if it meant that he would be able to play longer. "What do you have in mind?" he inquired cautiously.

Sir Jason appeared to be thinking deeply. "Shall we play for a kiss from Lady Diana?" he inquired at last. "I'll wager what I have against that, Glenwood."

"Dash it all, Sir Jason, you can't do that!" exclaimed Tommy, coloring. Turning to his father, he said, "Tell him that, sir!"

The earl, however, appeared lost in thought, staring at Derringer, whose face was dark with anger. "I did wager you the right to propose to see her here, Derringer, so I suppose this is nothing—"

Here he broke off, suddenly envisioning his daughter's expression should he lose—or should she hear of the wager. The game would scarcely be worth the candle. "No, we must think of something else," he announced reluctantly.

Sir Jason was staring at Derringer. "You won that, did you? But I see that the lady has not yet accepted your proposal."

"She refused me," said Derringer flatly. "As she should have, given the circumstances."

"Indeed?" murmured Sir Jason thoughtfully. "Well, Glenwood, for the moment perhaps we should forget including Lady Diana in our sport. Simply give me your voucher should you lose."

The earl, confident that he would win—for certainly he could redeem no voucher for the forseeable future, agreed and began another round.

By the time another hour passed, Sir Jason had won some five thousand pounds from the earl. Tommy, too, had lost a thousand. Rob was still asleep, and Derringer still had won most of his stack from Sir Jason.

The earl stared at his vouchers in disbelief. "Perhaps we shall have to play for a kiss from Diana," he murmured, half to himself.

"An excellent idea, Glenwood," Sir Jason exclaimed.

Tommy, staring at the voucher that he could not redeem until his birthday, did not protest this time. He and Derringer settled in to play seriously, for Derringer knew that there was no point in remonstrating with the earl in his present predicament. It was a marvel that any of Meadowbrook was left standing, reflected Derringer grimly as he watched the earl sign his chits.

The earl had lost twice more to Sir Jason, and Tommy was looking pale and more serious than Derringer had yet seen him. He now had vouchers for three thousand pounds on the table. It was abundantly clear that Diana had good reason to worry about Tommy and the effects of his father's gambling habits upon him.

Sir Jason, leaning back in his chair, stared at them benevolently. "Why not play one last hand? I shall make a special offer," he announced.

"Don't do it!" said Derringer firmly. "Walk away from the table now, Tommy!"

Here Sir Jason pushed the stack of money and chits from in front of him to the center of the table. "Why not play the last hand for everything? Winner takes all."

Tommy stared at him a moment, then at Derringer, swallowed convulsively, then pushed the little he had to the center with Sir Jason's. Derringer glanced at the earl, then went along with the others. The earl, last of all, began to move his bit to the middle.

"This time, Glenwood, instead of wagering a kiss from your lovely daughter, why not offer her hand in marriage?"

Tommy started to rise from his chair at this, but Derringer gestured to him to be seated. The earl, very pale and almost sober, nodded.

Sir Jason passed him a piece of paper. "Go ahead and write it out, leaving the winner's name blank," he commanded.

The earl did as he was bade, then closed his mind to further consequences and gave his attention to the game, as did the others. All was silent during the hand, save for the gentle snoring of Rob. Finally, it came round to Derringer, who had the last play.

"I believe, gentleman, that this mine," he announced, laying down a king and gathering in the money and chits from the middle of the table.

"I will write your name on the voucher," said the earl resolutely, reaching for it.

Silently the others watched him fill it in and hand it back to Derringer, who folded it and placed it with his winnings. The earl, who had risen from his place to write, walked slowly to the window and stared blindly into the darkness. Almost Derringer could have felt sorry for him. He had started to gather up his money when the earl sagged suddenly to the floor with a dull thud.

With Tommy, he hurried to the earl's side to check his heart and help him to a sofa. Rob still slept the sleep of the just, and Sir Jason didn't stir from the table. Instead, while the others were occupied with Lord Glenwood, he took advantage of the moment to substitute a blank piece of folded paper for the one giving Derringer the right to Lady Diana's hand in marriage.

By the time the others had revived the earl and gotten

back to the table, Sir Jason was gathering his belongings,
preparing to leave. Derringer swept all of the vouchers
from the table into his hand and carried them to the fire
that was still burning brightly in the morning room. After
tossing them in, he stood and watch them flame up briefly,
then turn to ash.

"You burned my vouchers as well as my father's and
sister's?" Tommy inquired a little shyly. When Derringer
nodded, he added, "That was very good of you, sir. Diana
wouldn't have liked that at all—nor did I."

Glancing across the room at the drawn face of the earl,
he said, "I don't believe even my father could stomach
that one. I daresay he would have had an apoplectic fit in
earnest if Diana had learned of it."

"That would be if she allowed him to live," observed
Derringer gravely, hoping to draw a smile from him.

Tommy responded, but the smile faded almost instantly.
"I cannot laugh, sir, for I should have been as responsible
as my father for her shame. I couldn't have held my head
up at all." He paused a moment, then added grimly, "And
what if the win had gone to Sir Jason?"

They were both silent for a moment, reflecting upon
how narrow their escape had been—although Derringer
himself had been certain enough that he could outflank
Sir Jason. Without his deck, Sir Jason was not as successful
a gambler as usual—certainly he had not his usual advantages.

Derringer liked the boy the better for his response, and,
awakening Rob, they adjourned to bed for the few hours
left of the night.

Only Sir Jason sat up a little later, a folded slip of notepaper between his fingers. He knew that Lady Diana had
a little money of her own from her grandmother's estate,
but he really had no interest in marrying her—humbling
her, yes—but marrying her, definitely not. Her brother

would very soon inherit a substantial fortune, and Sir Jason had hopes of making a large portion of that his own. Derringer's calm and forbidding presence had destroyed his hopes of that, however—at least temporarily.

He smiled to himself as he fingered the slip of notepaper. He could go to bed now, for he knew precisely what he was going to do to achieve his ends.

When Diana awoke the next morning, she felt an unaccustomed gladness sweep through her, and it took a moment to remember its source. As the memory of Derringer holding her in his arms returned, her cheeks grew warm and she hurried to rise from the bed, eager to see him once more. Tomorrow morning would be Valentine's Day, and she would be certain that the first male face she saw that morning was his. Then he would be her valentine for the duration of the year, and she would be his. And— if he had his way—tomorrow would be her wedding day. Derringer had sent his valet to Alex Worth in London yesterday afternoon, instructing him to see the Archbishop of Canterbury for a special license.

She dressed quickly but carefully, choosing a dress the color of fine claret and pulling her dark hair into a twist of curls. When she was satisfied with her reflection, she hurried from her room, closing the door carefully behind her.

As she turned to walk down the corridor, she saw a slip of paper on the carpet in front of her and stooped to pick it up. Unfolding it, she read the contents, written in an all-too-familiar scrawl: "John Derringer has my permission to marry my daughter, Lady Diana Crosswell." And her father had signed his name below it.

For a moment she stared at it, horror-stricken, then reread it, hoping that something would be different. It was terrible that her father would have put his name to such a chit, but it was unthinkable that John could have participated in such a wager after promising her that he would never do so again. And for what reason? She had accepted him. Had he made the wager before or after yesterday afternoon? She felt like a horse or a cow, to be sold to the highest bidder. As she considered this, a flash of anger revived her, making her feel less happy, but more herself again. Taking the note, she turned toward the stairs. It was time to put John Derringer in his place.

She had expected to see him in the dining room, but instead she met him as he was mounting the stairs. She froze in place as he approached her. So pleasant had his courtship been, so natural had it seemed to come to rely upon him, that for a moment she could not bear to think that she had misjudged him so badly. Staring down at his smiling face, she thought of the wager and her anger flamed anew.

"Good morning, love," he murmured as he drew close. "When shall we talk to your father about the wedding tomorrow?"

She glared at him. "About the wedding? Whose wedding would that be?" she demanded.

He stared at her, puzzled. "What's wrong, Diana?" he asked. "What has happened to make you so angry?"

"As though you don't know!" she exclaimed bitterly, waving the vowel in the air. "Wagering me as some sort of prize in a card game!"

"Yes, it was winner take all," announced Sir Jason gleefully from the bottom of the stairs. "I had hoped to win you myself, but as you see, it was Derringer who was the lucky man."

Caught by surprise, Diana turned abruptly toward Sir Jason, throwing herself off-balance. As she pitched forward, Derringer reached out to catch her and flung her back against the stairs. As she crouched there, she watched in horror as he lost his own balance and fell the length of the stairs to lie motionless at their base.

Diana managed to get to his side before the others arrived, drawn by her scream and the sound of the crash. Sir Jason stood to one side, making no move to help. His business had been completed.

Swiftly she oversaw having Derringer carefully moved to the nearest chamber, laying him flat on a board, for she was fearful that he had damaged his back or neck in the fall. Tommy raced off for the surgeon, saying that none of the stable boys could make the trip as quickly as he could on his hunter, and the earl hurried to bring his brandy from the study, ignoring Diana's comment that it would be useless since Derringer was unconscious. In the earl's eyes, brandy was never useless. In his view, even a slight sniff of it should have a beneficial effect. Rob stood at Diana's side, ready to run any errand she should appoint him.

Derringer himself lay without stirring, his face abnormally pale. Diana stroked his hair gently, murmuring to him all the while.

"This is all my fault, love," she said. "I should have thought before quarreling with you in such a place—or before quarreling with you at all. I don't care if you did win my hand in a card game. I would still marry you tomorrow."

Rob looked startled at her words, but for once he managed to keep his comments to himself, deciding instead to share them with Tommy upon his return.

It took some time for the surgeon to arrive, for he had been with another emergency case. He was a small, brisk man, and Diana watched him with a rising degree of confidence as he deftly checked the patient for broken bones.

"Will he be all right?" she asked at last, as he continued to probe and to listen to Derringer's chest.

The surgeon shook his head. "I think he will, Lady Diana, but I can't be certain. There are no broken bones, but he may have damaged himself internally, and I can't tell that as yet. He may be as right as rain except for being sore when he comes to or it may be—" Here he shrugged.

"When will you be able to tell?" she asked urgently.

The surgeon shrugged. "Perhaps if—" Here he glanced at Lady Diana and changed his wording. "Perhaps when he wakes up, we will know a little more."

With this she had to be satisfied, and she and Rob sat patiently by his side as the morning faded into the afternoon. There appeared to be no change in Derringer, but Diana comforted herself with the observation that his breathing was regular, and he appeared to be gaining color.

"I expect he will come to at any moment, Lady Diana," Rob assured her confidently, quite as though he had seen this kind of injury many times before.

And indeed, when the surgeon paid another call that afternoon, he said much the same thing as Rob, greatly to the latter's satisfaction.

The earl, in the meantime, had sought solace with his brandy, and had not been seen since the time he had produced a bottle of it for Derringer's use early in the morning. Tommy, upset by the accident and by the notion that the wager could have caused it, had retired to the library to play endless games of patience while he waited for news of Derringer's state. His restlessness wouldn't allow him to stay with Diana as Rob did, and once he had gone for the surgeon at breakneck speed, he had performed the only service that he could think of.

It was there that Sir Jason found him and invited him to a simple round of cards—no stakes—and to a glass or two of Blue Ruin, which he had had sent up from the Golden Rule.

By nine o'clock that evening, the gin had done its work, and Tommy was much the worse for wear. Sir Jason had seen to it that the card playing now had stakes, and Tommy, of course, was losing. After losing his pocket change and his watch, he agreed reluctantly to signing a voucher, this time for one hundred pounds.

"This is the last one," he assured Sir Jason as he signed his name on the bottom line and slumped over the table in a stupor.

"It is indeed," responded Sir Jason, pulling out the second slip under the voucher for one hundred pounds, which was still unsigned. The second slip, made out for fifty thousand pounds, payable at the time Tommy received his inheritance, was signed.

Pleased with himself, Sir Jason left Tommy slumped over the table, a victim of too much Blue Ruin, while he pocketed his voucher for fifty thousand pounds and prepared to depart. He had checked on his host earlier in the evening and found that the earl had already succumbed to his brandy and was sleeping the sleep of the dead. With Derringer still unconscious, it seemed unlikely that anyone else would interfere with him.

With that thought in mind, he gathered his belongings silently, sending his valet on ahead of him. In the corridor as he was departing he encountered Rob.

"Why are you leaving in the middle of the night, Sir Jason?" he inquired. "Aren't you going to stay? Derringer has waked up once and doubtless will again, very soon."

"Fascinating though that is," Sir Jason replied, "I believe that I will be able to tear myself away." He paused and looked about him. "Have all the servants gone to bed?" he inquired.

Rob nodded. "We're the only ones still about—well, us and Lady Diana."

"Is she still tending the patient?" asked Sir Jason.

Rob nodded again. "He was very glad to see her when he awoke, but he drifted away again almost immediately."

"What a waste of a woman," mused Sir Jason. "It does seem a pity to leave her like this." Staring at Rob for a moment, he said, "Mr. Wallace, come over here, please. I need your help to lift out a heavy box."

Trustingly Rob approached him as Sir Jason entered a nearby chamber and opened the door to a large wardrobe. Stepping inside as Sir Jason directed, Rob heard the door click closed behind him, and he found himself in darkness.

"Here now, Sir Jason!" he shouted. "Let me out of here right now! What do you mean by this kind of behavior?" Finally, when there was no response, his shouts died away as he sank to the floor and held his head in his hands, wondering what Sir Jason was up to that required his being out of the way.

After all, Sir Jason reasoned as he made his way toward the chamber where Derringer lay, he might as well enjoy himself—and certainly no one in the earl's family would ever mention that the Lady Diana, most cool and chaste and forbidding of all the young ladies of the *ton*, had suffered such a fate as he planned for her. To do so would place a period to any plan of marriage for her, should the chit ever decide to accept a husband.

Slipping quietly into John Derringer's room and moving softly behind the chair in which she sat drowsing, he quickly gagged her and tied her hands behind her. Angered by her struggling, he turned her round and looked her full in the eyes.

"Things will not go well for you, my girl, if you continue this way," he said grimly. "If you wish for things to turn a little ugly—perhaps I might rough up Derringer while he is still unconscious—go ahead and behave as you are."

At his words, Diana ceased to struggle and he was able to march her to the door. He removed her from Meadowbrook quickly enough in his closed carriage, which stood ready with the curtains tightly drawn, and only the driver, who was in his pay, to accompany him.

Tossing her casually onto the seat, he remarked, "Tomorrow will be Valentine's Day, Lady Diana. Assuredly mine will be the first face you will see. Is that not a delightful thought, my lady? You shall then think of me all the year long—and possibly longer," he added grimly.

A brief struggle answered his question and he smiled, enjoying her suffering. "Perhaps, Lady Diana, we should not wait until tomorrow morning?" he said softly. "After all, we are all alone in the carriage—although it would not, of course, be as comfortable as my bedchamber."

Diana grew perfectly still, and he laughed aloud. "What! No taste for love on the road, my lady? Perhaps you're right, though. This would be a most awkward affair. Better to wait."

At least she had delayed him for a little while, she thought miserably. Now she could only lie in the darkness, cursing her carelessness and laying her plans for defending herself. She also had more than enough time to think of John Derringer and to long for his presence as the carriage raced on through the night, carrying her to a decidedly unpleasant fate.

Back at Meadowbrook, Tommy awakened enough to realize that Sir Jason was no longer at the table with him and had departed with his money and his watch, but had left his unsigned vowel on the table. He stared at it foggily for a moment, wondering why he remembered having signed it when there clearly was no signature. Struggling to his feet, he staggered down the corridor toward the chamber where Derringer lay.

"Rob! Where the devil are you?" he called, holding his

head and wishing that he'd been bright enough to leave the Blue Ruin entirely alone.

A stacatto barrage of knocks answered his call, and he could faintly hear a muffled voice calling from a darkened room, "In here! In here!"

When he turned the key in the wardrobe, Rob sprang from it with alacrity. "I never realized before that I don't care for small, confined spaces, Tommy, but I can tell you now that I hate them! I was beginning to think that someday they'd find my bones in there when someone finally opened the thing."

"What were you doing in there, Rob?" demanded his friend. "That isn't where most people go to think."

"Well, of course not!" snapped the usually good-natured Rob. "It was your houseguest, the detestable Sir Jason Crume, that locked me in there!"

"Sir Jason!" exclaimed Tommy, staring at his friend. "Are you certain about that?"

Rob nodded emphatically. "I should say so! I suppose I can recognize the man as well as you."

"What I mean is," explained Tommy with an unwonted show of patience, "are you certain that it was he that closed the door? Why would he do such a thing?"

Rob shook his head. "I don't have any idea, but you can wager that he's up to no good. I mean, obviously if he locks me—"

He broke off as his words sank in. The two young men stared at each other. "Wager!" exclaimed Tommy. "It's Di he's after."

The two made the run to Derringer's chamber in record time, throwing open the door and staring in surprise at Derringer himself, who was sitting up in bed.

"Where is Di?" exclaimed Tommy, rushing into the room.

"That's what I was about to ask you," replied Derringer

in bewilderment. "I remember that she was here when I woke up earlier, but when I awoke just now, she was gone. Where could she be?"

Rob was staring at the floor. Leaning down, he picked up a locket, its thin gold chain snapped. Silently he held it up.

"Sir Jason's taken her," Tommy told Derringer bleakly. "He got me more than a little bosky and he locked Rob up. I'm sure my father is still drinking brandy in his room to celebrate an early Valentine's Day. He always has an excuse."

"Crume!" exclaimed Derringer, rising from his bed so suddenly that he sank back for a moment. "We have to follow them right away. We can't leave her with him or he'll see to it that she's ruined. His pride was a little damaged, I believe, when she preferred me to him."

With considerable effort, Derringer heaved himself to his feet, clutching at the bedpost for support.

"An understandable preference, I'm sure," murmured Rob consolingly, as he bustled about, laying out Derringer's clothes and his boots. A hasty inspection of the carriage tracks at the end of the drive indicated that Sir Jason was heading north, and that was confirmed by a nearby inn, where the carriage had paused to get a tankard of ale for the gentleman that had just begun his journey.

"In a fearful hurry, he were," observed the interested innkeeper. "The driver handed him his ale and they rattled off into the night with never a drink for the driver nor yet bait for the cattle."

He paused a moment, and when no more information was forthcoming, added inquisitively, "Friends of yours, governor?" to Tommy, who had questioned him.

"Hardly," returned Tommy briskly, wheeling his horse about and glaring at Rob to remind him that a lady's reputation was at stake and he could not indulge his desire to impart information. Derringer was clinging tightly to his horse and the world was still wheeling slightly for him as they rode on through the darkness.

It was an hour later and nearing dawn when they finally caught up with Crume at a rundown little inn. His carriage was parked in front, and they made their way silently to the back of the inn, hoping to take Sir Jason by surprise. They did, but not in the manner they had intended.

When Derringer, who had taken the lead, carefully opened the door to a back chamber, they entered to see Sir Jason neatly trussed and blindfolded and lying among the shards of a broken bottle. Next to him sat Diana.

"Why ever is he blindfolded, Diana?" asked her brother blankly as he hugged her to him. "Bound, yes—but blindfolded?"

Diana smiled and turned to John Derringer. "I was careful to tie him up and blindfold him before morning, and I have not looked at him since. Today is Valentine's Day, you know, sir. Or have you been away from England too long to remember?"

Derringer's eyes lit up. "And you did not care to have the gentleman as your valentine?" he inquired innocently. "At least you did not throw him down the stairs—he should count himself fortunate."

At this reminder of the accident she had caused, her eyes clouded and she looked down. Weakening in his resolve to punish her a little for it, he tilted her chin up so that she was looking into his eyes. "And who *is* the first gentleman that you've seen today, Lady Diana?" he inquired.

He held out his arms and she walked into them. Never had anyplace felt so much like home, she reflected.

Tommy looked on approvingly, but he added, "This is all very pretty, John, but if I were you, I'd be certain that my home had no stairs in it."

"A wise precaution," agreed his future brother-in-law.

"And I warn you, sir, that I shall expect you to live with us and I shall make life very hard for you."

Tommy grinned. "If I can take the governor, I can take you well enough, Derringer. It's Rob you'll have to worry about."

Rob looked shocked and hastened to disagree with his friend, assuring Derringer and Diana that he would be the soul of discretion whenever he came to visit.

The four of them prepared for their return to Meadowbrook, for as Tommy pointed out, the earl would soon discover that there was no one left there except himself, and he might eventually feel that something untoward had happened and worry about them.

"You know very well that he has never worried about anyone other than himself," pointed out his sister heartlessly.

Tommy nodded. "It's true, I know—but he does worry about us a little—at times when it costs him nothing financially or emotionally." As the events of the evening began to settle into a consistent picture for him, his brow creased and he pulled the unsigned voucher from his pocket to show to Derringer.

"I signed it, sure as fire," he said, "but there wasn't a signature to be seen."

Derringer nodded grimly, feeling quite certain that he knew what Sir Jason had done. "I'll just have a word with our guest before we drop him off with the local magistrate," he said.

To his surprise, Sir Jason was no longer in his small prison. His ropes had been cut and lay upon the floor, as did the kerchief that had gagged him.

"Gone," Derringer reported to them grimly when he returned to the others. They had borrowed a carriage, a rather old and rickety one, for Rob had agreed to drive Diana home. Derringer and Tommy hurried on ahead, anxious to be certain that all was well at Meadowbrook. The earl was there alone, to be sure, and they could not imagine just what Sir Jason had in mind, but the stableboy had indicated that Sir Jason had taken a horse and turned back in the direction he had come, leaving in a terrible hurry.

It was early morning when they arrived back at Meadowbrook, having encountered no sigh of Sir Jason. All appeared to be well there, and the two men looked at each other uneasily.

"What do you think he's up to?" asked Tommy. "He's a sneaksby rather than a man of courage, so whatever he would do would be underhanded.

Suddenly Derringer clapped his hand to his forehead. "Diana! If I had my wits about me, I would never have left her!" And he turned his horse back in the direction of the inn where they had found her.

"Di?" yelled Tommy as he galloped along beside him. "Do you mean he was lying in wait for her?"

"He must have suspected that we might separate after he escaped. What a fool I was not to suspect this!"

"Well," shouted Tommy comfortingly, "at least she has Rob with her."

Derringer, who could find no comfort in the protection that the slender Rob might be able to offer her, rode all the harder, picturing the worst that could happen and wishing that he had his hands about Sir Jason's throat. When the arrived at the inn where they had first found Diana and Sir Jason, there appeared to be no one there; nor was there any sign of their quarry. Seeing a cart filled with hay moving slowly down the road, the two of them hurried over to it.

"Have you passed a carriage since you've been on the road this morning?" demanded Tommy of the tall, thick youth driving the cart.

The boy looked down at Tommy blankly, his blue eyes showing little sign of understanding, although he did bring the cart to a halt.

"I say, have you passed a carriage this morning?" he asked again, raising his voice as though the boy might be deaf.

Very slowly the boy began to nod his head. "Aye," he replied, preparing to goad his ox into motion again.

"What did the people look like who were in it?" asked Tommy impatiently.

The boy stopped again and appeared to be considering the matter carefully.

Unable to wait any longer, Tommy exploded. "Were there two men and a young woman?" he asked. "One of the men in black?"

After a moment more, the boy again began to nod.

"Have you come far since you saw them?" asked Tommy, eager for more information.

"Never mind waiting for the answer," urged Derringer. "We don't have any time to lose. We'll have to trust that the boy really saw them." In his heart, however, he felt that it was all too likely that the boy understood little of what they had said to him.

Together they raced down the narrow lane. They both knew that their mounts wouldn't last long at the rate they were going, and they had no idea how much farther they might have to go nor if they would be able to find other horses when they needed them, but desperation drove them. Derringer was keenly aware, too, that he had fallen a full flight of stairs yesterday. The pain in his side grew sharper as they rode, and his head roared with a sound that was not due to the wind.

A few minutes later they saw another cart approaching them, this time a small donkey cart driven by two young girls. Derringer and Tommy slowed abruptly, apologizing for the stir of dust they had caused and explaining their plight.

"Have you seen such a carriage?" asked Derringer, after Tommy had described it and its occupants.

Both girls nodded, their eyes wide. The older one held out a claret-colored ribbon. "The lady dropped this out of the carriage as they drove by," she said shyly.

Derringer felt his breath catch. Diana had still been wearing the claret gown from yesterday, having never gone to bed last night.

"Was it very long ago that you saw them?" demanded Tommy, also recognizing the ribbon.

"Not more than a mile back," announced the older one. She looked up at them with bright eyes. "The lady was very pretty," she informed them, "but she looked tired and dusty."

"Thank you, ladies!" called Tommy, as they dug their heels into the sides of their weary mounts and resumed the quickest speed they could manage, cursing Sir Jason all the while.

The girls were quite accurate it appeared, for they had gone no more than a mile when they saw the carriage in the distance, listing to one side with a broken axle. Tommy and Derringer could see that there were figures seated beside it, but they could distinguish no more than that.

As they grew closer, however, they could see that all three of them were there and that they were deeply absorbed in whatever it was that they were doing, so deeply in fact that Diana and Rob didn't at first hear the approach of the horses.

Derringer and Tommy drew up beside them and looked at one another in amazement. The three of them were playing cards, although Sir Jason was somewhat handi-capped by the cords that bound his wrists and his ankles.

Rob looked up at them and waved, Diana blew a kiss,

then they promptly returned to their play. Sir Jason acknowledged them with the slightest of sardonic bows.

Diana threw down the last card and pulled the stack of gold and notes in the middle toward her. "Remember, Sir Jason, it was winner take all. Do you recall? And he was playing for his freedom, of course," she said to the newcomers, rising stiffly to turn and lean her head against Derringer's leg as he sat upon his horse.

"I would get down and hug you, my dear," he said, looking down at her fondly, "but I don't think I'm capable of doing so just now."

His comment brought on a flurry of activity as Tommy and Rob attempted to help him step down from the horse.

"I would offer to help, of course," observed Sir Jason, "but I fear that you would have to release me in order for me to be of much use."

"That's quite all right, old man," said Tommy dryly. "You're not going to be unbound for quite some time. The local magistrate will take care of you."

"I've been thinking about that, Tommy," said Diana slowly. "I know precisely what Sir Jason had in store for me, but he wasn't able to bring it about, you know." She glanced at him contemptuously. "Indeed, I doubt if he would have been able to even if I had not disarmed him on both occasions."

She put her arms about her brother. "Just think of the ridiculous stir it will make it this gets about," she said persuasively. "As it is, we have the vowel that our father gave to John promising my hand in marriage, and we have the vowel you signed after too much Blue Ruin, allowing him fifty thousand pounds of your money. He has nothing in hand any longer that can cause us any harm, and who would ever believe his pitiful story, even if he were willing to tell it and bear the disgrace of being defeated twice by a woman."

Rob cleared his throat, and she added, "Once by a woman and once by a couple."

"You are entirely correct, dear lady," agreed Sir Jason. "I cannot think that you could have put it more convincingly. What need is there, after all, to drag your dirty linen through the streets? Least said, soonest mended."

Tommy stared at him in distaste. "Couldn't we at least drag him along behind the carriage on the way home?" he inquired hopefully.

His sister shook her head. "It would stir up an undue amount of dust," she pointed out. "He is not worth the trouble."

Sir Jason again nodded emphatically. "You are an eminently sensible woman, Lady Diana."

"If you agree with me once more, Sir Jason," she returned briskly, "I will know that I am wrong, and I will leave you to Tommy."

Sir Jason lapsed into an immediate and prolonged silence, watching Tommy warily.

"Are you quite all right?" inquired Derringer tenderly, putting his arms around Diana and trying not to wince as she hugged him.

"Of course I am. After all, Rob was here with me, and we really handled it all quite nicely."

"That's what I would like to hear," said Tommy. "How in thunder did you and Rob manage to get away from Sir Jason when he had a gun?"

"We could hear him coming, naturally," replied his sister. "We had been certain that he would follow us at some point. Rob parked the carriage behind a hedge so that Sir Jason couldn't see us as we took the spindle off the axletree. Then it looked as though we had broken down. Rob hid inside the carriage and I waited outside so that I could hug him."

"Hug him!" exclaimed her brother, revolted. Even

Derringer looked a little taken aback. "Why would you hug a snake?"

"So that he doesn't bite you," responded his sister promptly. "He thought that I had grown hysterical because of the accident and being alone. I told him that Rob had gone for help."

She frowned down at Sir Jason. "I couldn't believe that you would think me so completely helpless, but it certainly worked to our advantage, for Rob was able to surprise him and take his gun quite easily."

Sir Jason shrugged. "I admit it. I underestimated you badly—but I never will again, dear lady."

"There won't be an 'again'," she responded promptly.

By the time the weary little group arrived home in the rickety carriage (which had been repaired by the enterprising Rob), everyone was tired to the point of the exhaustion.

To their surprise, the earl was waiting for them on the front steps, eager to learn what had taken place. Watching Derringer dismount stiffly, accompanied by Diana—who did look as though she had been dragged behind the carriage—his dismay was clear. It became still more clear when Sir Jason emerged, wrists and ankles still bound.

"You should be horsewhipped, sir!" the earl announced. "And I shall see to it!"

"No, you'll not make more of a stir about this, Father," Diana informed him. "We have already discussed this and decided it will be best if Sir Jason goes on about his way— not our way, of course, for we expect never to see him again."

"And will shoot him on sight if we do!" added Tommy grimly.

Derringer, recognizing the good sense of Diana's argument and the fact that it would be her reputation that would be muddied, reluctantly cut the cords on Sir Jason's bonds—although still longing to separate that gentleman into two or three pieces before parting with him.

He had been gone no longer than ten minutes when Alex Worth arrived, bearing the special license. He was ushered into the drawing room, where sat all of the group, in various stages of disarray.

Worth looked at them in astonishment, particularly when Derringer got up to welcome him and could scarcely walk across the room.

"What has happened to you, John?" he demanded, looking about him. "What has happened to all of you?"

"We are in love, Alex," Derringer announced with a grin, circling Diana with one bruised arm. Diana stood there proudly, her claret gown now a dusty gray, its skirt and bodice torn. "Are we not, my dear?" he asked softly, looking down into her eyes as she nodded. "Do you mind terribly that my eyes aren't blue?"

She shook her head. "It may take its toll in later years of course," she added, "but I shall try to rise above it. After all, when you love someone, you must take him as he is."

"Well, speaking of that," said Alex, who felt that they had all run mad, "are you not planning to have your marriage today—on Valentine's Day?"

The happy couple nodded and the rest of the group appeared to be gratified by this plan, but no one moved, all of them except the earl exhausted beyond belief.

"Then don't you think that it would be as well to tidy up just a little before the ceremony?" he inquired delicately. "The minister will arrive soon, just as you requested, John."

Derringer shook his head. "If I went upstairs to clean up for my wedding, Alex, I should never be able to get back down. It has been an exceedingly difficult day."

Alex swallowed. "I believe that I can see that," he agreed, "but it does seem that on your wedding day—"

Derringer interrupted him. "Alex, look at Lord Glenwood. Is he not impeccable?"

The earl, pleased to have this pointed out, stood so that Alex could have the full benefit of his sartorial splendor.

"Yes, of course he looks very elegant, but—"

"Lord Glenwood will give the bride away, Alex. Keep the minister's attention focused on him. Diana and I will do our best to stand there and look as though we have not been three weeks away from soap and water. Tommy and Rob will stand up with us and lend us moral support."

He paused and looked at the two young men. "Also, if they stand close enough to us, we will look quite tidy in comparison. It will all work out, Alex."

He pulled Diana even closer to him, trying not to groan in pain as he did so, and said to Alex, "You told me that I would never be the same if I came to Meadowbrook. I had no idea that you were a fortune-teller."

Bending to kiss her, he murmured, "I believe, ma'am, that this kiss is mine."

"I believe that you are quite correct, sir," she returned. Smiling, she smoothed his hair gently back from his face and lifted her lips to his.

It would have been difficult to determine who was the happiest that afternoon—for Sir Jason was a free man, the earl had finally managed to marry into money, Tommy was to have a brother-in-law he could respect and love, Rob had managed to rescue his beloved Lady Diana, and Lady Diana and John Derringer had found a deep and abiding love.

As the sun slipped over the horizon and the candles were lighted at Meadowbrook, Diana and John repeated their vows. Despite their stiffness and exhaustion, each was aware of the strong current that vibrated between them.

Once the ceremony was over and the earl had toasted them, John offered his arm to his wife.

"Would you care for a stroll through the maze, Mrs. Derringer?"

"Have you lost your mind, John?" exploded Alex. "It's cold and getting dark and you can scarcely move!"

Tommy elbowed him sharply, and even Rob frowned at him. "Lovers, you know," he murmured in a low voice that carried halfway across the room.

Tommy chuckled. "It's an adaptation of Sir Jason's favorite game—"Winner take all.""

A Valentine from Venus

Cindy Holbrook

Chapter 1

"I swear by Zeus himself, but it is cold," a tall, fatally beautiful woman said as she floated, rather than walked, along the elegant street of Mayfair. She shivered. The fact she wore the flimsiest of Grecian draperies, along with delicate golden sandals, might have had something to do with it.

"You really should stop swearing," a short man said. He bounded beside the stunning woman. His blue eyes twinkled merrily as he glanced around. A passing pedestrian passed through him, literally.

She laughed. "You know I'm Father's pet. Besides, I doubt he'd hear me in this gods-forsaken land."

"It's called England," Cupid said.

"You may call it what you wish," Venus said, with an elegant shrug. "I will call it what I wish."

"I enjoy a visit here every once in a while. It is always such a change in routine. Ah, here we are," Cupid said, halting before an impressive town house. His eyes sparkled all the more, and a cherubic grin crossed his face. "The Marquis of Waverly's. Shall we?"

"Of course," Venus said, sighing.

In a glimmer they appeared in a library. A tall, brown-haired man, with brown eyes, sat at a desk, a book before him. Beside him sat a petite woman, a pen in hand and a tablet upon her lap. Her black hair was toppled into a semblance of a bun. More strands straggled from the imperfect mass than were confined. Both inhabitants wore sober, serious expressions.

Venus strolled about them, studying them. "So these are the two."

"Yes," Cupid said, bouncing upon the balls of his feet. "These are the two."

"Whatever are they wearing?" Venus asked, a disapproving frown marring her brow. "There are so many layers."

"They dress for the climate."

"Well, they most certainly do not dress for love," Venus said, her tone dry.

"Amelia," the man exclaimed. "I do not understand. How is this Byron so popular?"

"I do not know, Michael," Amelia answered, shaking her head, the blue of her eyes dark with confusion.

"Who is Byron?" Venus asked.

"A man after your own heart," Cupid said. "His affair with the Lady Caroline Lamb is notorious."

"Indeed?" Venus's face brightened perceptibly. "Do show me this man."

"No," Cupid said. "These are the two. Byron doesn't require your assistance."

Venus lifted her brow. "Everyone can use my assistance!"

"Only look at this," Michael said, jabbing a finger at the open book. "He has left out both a comma and a period."

"Indeed," Amelia said, leaning forward to study the page.

Venus strolled over to read at a glance the entirety of *Childe Harold*. "How amusing. Tormented and passionate. I love it."

Amelia sighed, drawing back with a frown. "I can never understand how he has become published, let alone become so popular."

"I know," Michael said, slamming the book shut. "They reject my works for this . . . this tripe!"

Venus stiffened. She turned a narrowed green gaze upon Cupid. "No! It is impossible!"

Cupid smiled. His cherubic face held a definite look of satisfaction, bordering upon that of malice. "You bet me you could bring any two people of my choosing together. Well, here they are, my chosen couple."

"They do not deserve love," Venus said. "They read such poetry and call it tripe! They look for commas and such. They see with their eyes, and not with their hearts."

"Everyone deserves love," Cupid said, turning sober. "And they do love each other."

"Oh, I can see the passion," Venus said with an ungodesslike snort.

"There are many forms of passion," Cupid said. "Amelia is not Cleopatra and Michael is not Marc Antony . . ."

"Cleo and Marc," Venus said, a fond smile curving her lips. "How I loved them."

"But that does not mean they have no passion," Cupid continued with a frown.

"Ha!" Michael said, shoving Bryon's work aside. "I know I can write better than this."

Venus threw up her hands. "No! I refuse to waste my efforts upon this human."

"Then I win the bet." Cupid smiled in triumph. "And you must acknowledge I am the better."

Venus rolled her divine eyes. "I should never have drank so much ambrosia punch that night."

"*I* have brought just as difficult a couple together," Cupid said, clearly taunting. "They still live happily here in England."

"Do they?" Venus asked. Her tone lacked enthusiasm.

"Yes," Cupid nodded. He laughed. "But you wouldn't have heard of them. Neither have killed for the other, or killed themselves because of love."

Venus yawned. "How dull and boring."

"That is your problem, Mother," Cupid said. "If it is common, everyday love, you are uninterested."

Venus's brow shot up. "That is because I am not an everyday goddess!"

"But there is something to be said for that kind of love," Cupid said, almost musingly. "Something totally satisfying in matching two people together and knowing their love will survive the mundane day-by-day of life."

"I can't believe you are my son sometimes," Venus muttered, shaking her head. "You used to be such a delightful imp. Whatever happened to you?"

"Age, Mother," Cupid said, his tone dry.

"I am far older than you," Venus said. "And I have never become so . . . so ordinary."

Cupid pinned her with a steady gaze. "Then you withdraw from the bet?"

Venus glanced at Amelia and Michael, whose heads were once again bowed over their respective work. "Only look at them. They do not even have a spark in them."

"They are humans," Cupid said. "You know each and every one of them is born with a spark inside. But these two will never know it, if you do not bring them together before Valentine's Day."

"And why," Venus asked, her eyes narrowing, "did you set that particular day?"

"Because . . ." Cupid halted. It seemed he listened a moment and then smiled. "Only wait. You will see."

"My lord," a female voice called, and the door to the library opened. A tall, voluptuous redheaded woman entered. Her green frock was the height of fashion and showed her excellent figure to perfection.

"Hm?" Michael asked, looking up. He blinked. "Oh, hello, Estelle."

Estelle put her hands to her hips. "Your butler did not inform you that Mother and I had arrived for tea?"

Michael blinked, utter bewilderment washing his face . . . "I-I don't know." His gaze turned in appeal to Amelia. "Did Belton tell us that?"

"I-I do not remember. P-perhaps he did," Amelia stammered. She turned a contrite gaze upon the woman. "I am terribly sorry, Estelle, but we . . . I don't recall."

"I will come immediately . . ." Michael said quickly, as Estelle's face darkened. He sprang from his chair, sheets of paper flying in all directions.

"No," Estelle said, her tone brisk. "Tea is quite over, and I have no further time."

"Who is she?" Venus asked, her eyes narrowing. "She reminds me of Juno."

"I only came to remind you about the Harpers' ball tonight," Estelle said.

"The Harpers' ball?" Michael asked.

"I knew you would forget!" Estelle cried. "No matter. I've already talked to your valet. He knows exactly what you are to wear."

"H-he does?" Michael asked.

"Yes," Estelle said. "I'll not have you wearing that shabby, brown jacket you wore to the Springdales' last Thursday. The Harpers' ball begins at eight o'clock. You will come to my house an hour early to escort me."

"Er, yes, of course," Michael said, his face turning red.

"I've already apprised your coachman of your sched-
ule," Estelle said. She turned to leave, and then turned
back, bending a strict frown upon Michael and Amelia.
"And I'll not have you two talking all evening about books
and whatnot. I don't mind that you two remain holed up
here every day scribbling away, but I won't have it at the
ball. People are beginning to think you are eccentric,
Michael." She then gazed at Amelia and glanced away, as
if making any comment upon her was completely unneces-
sary. "Be sure to pay attention tonight, Michael." With
that, Estelle left the library.

"She does remind me of Juno," Venus said, a spark
entering into her eyes. "Who is she? Surely not his
mother."

"No," Cupid said. "She is his fiancée."

Venus's brow shot up. "Great Zeus!"

"Their marriage will be upon Valentine's Day."

"Ah," Venus said, nodding. She frowned. "What is this
Valentine's Day?"

"The one day they celebrate love."

"Only one day?" Venus asked. Her brow rose. "And you
choose to visit this place? They should have feasts and
celebrations for love year-round."

Cupid shook his head. "They have but the one day."

"Well," Venus said, "at least these two have chosen the
correct day."

"He chose the date," Cupid said. "Not she."

"I see," Venus murmured. She studied Amelia and
Michael again with a contemplative frown.

Michael shifted upon his feet. "I-I had best, er, go."

"Oh, yes," Amelia said, gathering up her own materials
and standing.

"Do you attend the Harpers' ball?" Michael asked.

"I think I do." Amelia's brow wrinkled. "Mother mentioned it, I believe."

"Then I will see you there."

"Yes," Amelia said, nodding. She scurried toward the door, Michael striding behind her. "Do not worry about seeing me out, you'd best . . . best attend Estelle."

"Yes," Michael murmured as they departed the room.

Venus stared after them, still frowning. Cupid smiled a knowing smile. "Well, Mother. Do you think you can do it?"

Venus's gaze returned to him. Her chin lifted imperiously. "I have not divined if your Amelia and Michael have the spark in them or not. But I know for certain that Estelle does not. I recognize such a creature very well."

"Yes," Cupid said, nodding. "But I believe Michael and Amelia will surprise you. They do love each other, they just don't know it."

Venus smiled. "In that case . . ."

"No," Cupid said quickly. "Part of the bet is that you must do this without casting your love spell. You can contrive and advise, but you mustn't just bespell them."

Venus grimaced. "Ever since you've given up your bow and arrow, you have become positively tedious."

"They must come to know they love each other upon their own," Cupid said, frowning. "Spells do not last forever."

"Oh, very well," Venus conceded. "I'll do it your way."

"If you can remember how to do so," Cupid said, his eyes taking on a twinkle again.

"Do not be impertinent," Venus scolded. "I am still the Goddess of Love. If you wish me to waste my talents upon these two, so be it. With or without my spells it will be child's play."

Amelia moved through the figures of the country dance, her mind churning over a verse of Michael's poem which they had been working upon that day. She took her partner's hand, a Lord Durby, no, it must be Darby. "I love you . . ." she murmured.

"Y-you d-do?" Lord Darby exclaimed, a look of astonishment crossing his rather thin, horsey face.

"I love you . . ." Amelia repeated again to herself.

"I say," Lord Darby said, blinking. "I'd no notion."

"Like . . . like what?" Amelia asked herself.

"Like what?" Lord Darby asked, frowning.

"I don't know." Amelia sighed. "It must be like something."

The figures of the dance divided them at the moment. She noticed inconsequentially that Lord Darby all but plowed into the woman before him. He certainly wasn't an apt dancer. Her mind worked on the more difficult issue at hand. Like what? The sun? The moon? The stars? Amelia frowned, deep in concentration. "Like the ocean . . . loves the shore . . . and . . . ?"

Once again Lord Darby and she drew together. She curtsied deeply to him, immediately knowing the answer. "No, no more need be said."

"It doesn't?" Lord Darby asked, frowning. "But if you love . . ."

"No and . . . it's period," Amelia said, feeling totally satisfied. "The end." Lord Darby looked as if he begged to differ. At least his look of confusion rather than agreement made Amelia think so. "You must agree. Anything more would be superfluous and trite."

"T-trite?" Lord Darby asked, sounding offended.

"Truly," Amelia nodded, surprised to discover Lord Darby was a man to hold such strong views upon literature. "It's always important to know when to end it."

"End it?" Lord Darby asked, his voice rising. "But Madame, I thought we just began it!"

"You must be the proponent of the long form," Amelia

said, her tone soothing. "I fear I am not." The strains of the music ended. Amelia smiled. "Thank you for the dance and the discussion."

In truth, now that she had decided upon the stanza, she could not wait to go to Michael and discover what he thought. She curtsied and turned quickly from Lord Darby. She thought she heard him mutter, "Shortest damn affair I've ever had." But she didn't wait or think another thing of it.

She wended her way through the crowd, spying Michael, just then leading Estelle from the dance floor. She rushed up to them.

"Hello, Estelle," Amelia said, breathlessly. She turned her gaze to Michael in excitement. "Michael, I've thought it out! I love you like the ocean loves the shore. Period. That's it."

"What?" Estelle exclaimed.

"Michael's eyes lighted and he reached a hand out to her. "Amelia, that is wonderful."

"Wonderful?" Estelle exclaimed. Her gaze flicked about and a deep flush reddened her face.

Only then did Amelia notice she'd drawn no small attention. Those surrounding them stared at her with mouths agape. She thought she heard old Lady Henderson mutter, "Brash, hussy," but she wasn't certain.

Amelia flushed. "I'm sorry, Estelle. I know you didn't want Michael and me to discuss this in public, but I—I fear I became overly excited."

"But it's excellent," Michael stated, his tone approving. "I like it very much."

Old Lady Henderson cackled. "Course he would. Young rake."

Estelle glared at Michael, as if she'd relish kicking him. She then turned a bright smile upon Lady Henderson and the others. "You must forgive Amelia and Michael. They but discuss a poem they have been working upon. Th-they are writers, you know.''

"A poem, you say?'' Lady Henderson asked, her mouth working in disbelief.

"But of course," Amelia said, frowning. "What else would . . ." She halted. A deep blush covered her. "Oh, you thought that I . . . I meant it. That I was declaring . . . oh, dear. No." She shook her head vehemently. "I-I never meant . . ." She stopped and stared at those who stared at her. Her native intelligence, now free of its muse, warned her that anything else she said would only succeed in deepening the pit she'd already dug. Period. That's it. She nodded her head. "If you will excuse me."

She turned quickly and scurried across the ballroom to where her mother sat. Mortification engulfed her. What a fool she had made of herself. She slowed her pace when she approached her mother. A woman sat beside her. One of the most fatally beautiful women she had never seen. Hers was the face to make one wish to write poetry to her. Indeed, her beauty was such that she seemed otherworldly.

"Oh, dearest," Lady Thornton exclaimed. "Do come here and meet Venitia Lovall. She and I are having the most intriguing conversation. I feel like we have been friends for years. Silly, but it's true."

Amelia flushed even more deeply. If her mother counted this woman as a friend, then no doubt she had already bent the poor woman's ear off about Amelia's sad plight. Her mother rarely had any conversation other than that of her daughter's unwed state. "I see."

"Do have a seat, Amelia," Venitia said, her green eyes laughing. "I hope you do not mind if I call you by name. As your mother said, I feel already as if we are close friends."

Amelia sighed and sat down. "Indeed."

"Well," Lady Thornton said, fluttering her fan. "I do believe I will go and talk to Lady Sotherford. Amelia, you and Venetia can then have a pleasant coze." She stood abruptly and hastened away.

Amelia peeked at the woman. The woman was studying her quietly, almost as if she were looking into her mind. Amelia smiled in embarrassment. "I have no doubt Mother has instructed you upon what you should say to me."

The woman's brow rose. She laughed. "You are very intelligent, my dear. Perhaps too intelligent for your own good."

"Yes," Amelia nodded. "That has often been said of me."

"Really?" Venitia said, her eyes twinkling. "Well, I won't tell you all the things that have been said about me. Even when they are true, they are not always welcoming."

Amelia's eyes widened and a laugh escaped her. "I cannot believe anyone would say anything bad about you."

"Oh, I've created my . . . er, 'scandals.' Is that not the term you use here in England?"

"Yes? Then you are not from here?"

"No," Venitia said. She waved a hand. "I'm from Greece . . . Rome, what have you and when have you."

"Truly?" Amelia asked, intrigued. She had never been outside of London. "You've been to both those places?"

"I'd prefer to think that I am both those places," Venetia said, smiling. "But then my son has often said I have far too much pride in such matters."

"I see," Amelia said with a hesitancy. She suddenly felt as if she were deeper into a conversation than she knew, and far, far out of her depth.

A look of surprise crossed the woman's face. "You are intelligent. Do not let it worry you, my dear. I will not harm you. I promise."

For some reason, that statement eased Amelia's mind greatly. It had been but a flashing thought, but she did

have the strongest feeling she would not care to have this
woman set against her. "Thank you."

"Don't thank me yet," Venitia said. "That will be for
later." She looked directly at Amelia. "Your mother is
concerned you have not yet married."

Amelia stiffened. "She need not worry. I . . . I do not
wish to marry."

"No," Venitia said. "You see no reason to do so, I
believe."

A warmth rushed through Amelia. Finally, someone who
understood her. "That is it! I know Mother says I am on
the shelf, which I imagine I am, but I-I see no reason why
I must wed. I am happy with my life the way it is."

"You are?"

"Yes, I am," Amelia said defiantly. Venitia only gazed
at her with a knowing look. The wind promptly wheezed
from Amelia's sail and she sighed. "Besides, I am not a
woman who—who attracts men."

"Why not?"

"Because"—Amelia flushed—"I-I am not beautiful, like
you are. And I'm blue."

Venitia's brows shot up. "Your complexion is quite perfect from what I can see."

"No," Amelia laughed. "I mean I am a bluestocking. I
read, and write and study literature. Men do not . . . they
do not care for women like me."

"Ah, I see." Venitia cocked her head. "Lord Waverly
likes you, I believe?"

"Of course. But his interests run in the same direction
as mine. And we've been friends since childhood."

"So your mother told me," Venitia said. "What happens
when Lord Waverly weds?"

Amelia blinked. "I beg your pardon?"

"I asked, what will you do when he weds Miss Carstair?"

Amelia's heart began to pound for no reason at all. "I do not understand."

"Once he is wed," Venitia said, almost with the tone of one talking to a slow-witted child, "things will change. You and he cannot spend all your time together. Marriage will change all that." She laughed. "And if it didn't, Miss Carstair would be certain to change it."

"I don't think Estelle minds our . . . our studies," Amelia said. Even she noticed the thread of hesitancy in her voice.

"That is because she does not have the ring on Waverly's finger yet," Venitia purred. "When she does, she'll bring down the whip. As you would say here in England. I've noticed many of your sayings deal much with animals and the training of them."

"I beg pardon?" Amelia asked, blinking.

"Bring to heel, light hand upon the reins, and such," Venitia said, waving a white hand. "Far too confining. As stifling as these clothes." She shifted, as if terribly uncomfortable. "A great deterrent to passion no doubt."

Amelia blinked, and tried to stifle her gurgle of embarrassment. "Er, yes. I suppose."

"As I was saying," Venitia said. "Miss Carstair will certainly bring down the whip. She will have Michael ruled. That is the creature's nature."

"D-do you think so?" Amelia asked, blanching. The vision which flashed before her was not a pleasant one.

"You love him, don't you?"

"What?"

"You love Lord Waverly, do you not?"

"No," Amelia said quickly. "Of course not." She flushed. She couldn't believe news could have traveled so fast, but perhaps it had. "If you mean about what I said to him . . . a little while before, that was all a misunderstanding. I . . . we had been working on a piece of poetry

and . . . and I . . . what I said was to be a line from it. I . . .
I was not telling him I loved him."

"Actually, I had not meant that," Venitia said. "But may
I suggest you stop working so hard on the poetry and start
bending that intelligence of yours to life." Her smiled
turned whimsical. "They always suggest you write what you
know the most about, do they not? You do wish to write
about love."

Amelia flushed to her toes. "I do not love Michael. I
mean, not in that . . . manner."

Venitia laughed. "In what manner?"

"You know what I mean," Amelia said, her voice low.

"Oh, I know what you mean." Venitia smiled. "In fact,
I would say I've written the book on the subject. My question is, do *you* know what you mean?" She rose. "You
know, Nero fiddled while Rome burned. That wasn't just
a story. He actually did. Of course, he wasn't too bright at
any time. Not at all intelligent like you are. But he fiddled
because he didn't know what else to do. If you will excuse
me. I have other matters to attend. But I shall be around,
if I can be of any service to you."

Amelia stared after Venitia Lovall, feeling as if in one
conversation, the woman had set off several large explo-
sions. Her gaze turned toward Michael, and her heart
caught. She couldn't be in love with him. If she were in
love with him, what would happen in the future once he
was married? Remaining firmly planted on the shelf had
not seemed such a lonely prospect until now.

Was Venitia right? Was her world going up in flames
about her and she just hadn't known it?

Michael shuffled through the buffet line behind Estelle.
His mind was bent upon Amelia's words. "I love you like
the ocean loves the shores." Period. That's it.

He scooped a large helping of something upon his plate. It would work. For the piece, it would truly work. He leaned over and forked some prawns upon his plate and the red sauce beside it.

"I have been thinking about our honeymoon," Estelle said as she delicately spooned fresh green beans in a cream sauce upon her plate.

Michael frowned. "Is ocean the best choice though?"

"Ocean?" Estelle asked. "We are not going to the ocean."

"Water, perhaps?" Michael murmured, still in brown study.

"No," Estelle said. "I thought we would visit my aunt in Lancashire. She is very, very influential in political circles. You are going to take up your seat in the House, are you not?"

"Ocean," Michael said. "It's still better."

"Period. That's it." Michael nodded.

Estelle smiled. "I am so glad you agree with me."

Michael's survival instinct brought him back to heel very quickly. "What, my dear?"

Estelle frowned. "I said I am glad you agree with me that we shall go to my aunt's for the honeymoon. I am sure it would be a perfect opportunity for you to meet the men who can further your career most."

Michael's heart sank. He very well knew she wasn't talking about publishers. Publishers from Fleet Street would never be invited to visit her prominent aunt. "I . . . I agreed to that?"

"Yes, you just did," Estelle said, her brilliant eyes narrowing.

Michael forced a weak smile. "Then that is what we shall do."

"Why?" Estelle asked. "What were you talking about?"

"Oh, nothing."

"What were you talking about?" Estelle repeated, her beautiful eyes becoming piercing gimlets.

"I'm sorry," Michael said, realizing there was nothing to do now but confess. "I . . . I was only debating if water might not be as good a word as ocean for the poem Amelia and I have been writing."

Estelle halted. "I was talking about our honeymoon! I cannot believe you are still thinking about that."

"But I think Amelia is right," Michael said.

"I don't want to hear about Amelia or your silly verse," Estelle said slowly, her eyes flashing. "Now that is enough. Pay attention."

"Yes, Estelle," Michael said quietly.

He tried his level best to pay attention to the conversation once Estelle and he sat down at the table next to Lady and Lord Carstair. Lady Carstair was still a handsome woman, though her hair was not as glossy as Estelle's or her face as well drawn. Lord Carstair was a small man, with nervous twitches that seemed to streak through his body randomly. He rarely had a word to say for himself, or for anything else for that matter.

Michael nodded to Lord Carstair, who gave him a quick smile, and then turned his attention back to his food. The conversation appeared to be upon some jacket Prinny had worn and what the Beau had said about it. Everyone was laughing over the quip, so Michael laughed as well, absently dipping a prawn in the red sauce and eating it.

"Blast and damn!" he exclaimed. He had not noticed that the prawn was still in its shell. Prawns were always shelled, weren't they? Worse, the red sauce indeed was a currant jam. He detested currant jam above all things!

Every one halted, staring at him. Michael stared back.

"Water," he muttered, attempting the word around the disgusting mouthful of crustacean shell and tart jam. He looked around. Why was there no glass of water?

"Not that again!" Estelle exclaimed. "You promised you were not going to think about your writing."

"No," Michael said, feeling himself turn blue. He couldn't eat the concoction at the moment.

"I think . . ." Lord Carstair said, his tone diffident, "th-that he wants a glass of water."

"Be quiet, Hubert," Lady Carstair said sharply. "This is between Estelle and Michael."

Michael gagged. If he didn't do something swiftly, the thing which would be between him and Estelle would be a mouthful of crusty, currant prawn.

"Excushe me," he said with as much dignity as he could. He stood and strode from the dining room. He entered the hall and looked about desperately. He spotted a potted fern and went swiftly over to it. He bent and spit out the disgusting mass into the plant.

Sighing, he turned and then stepped backwards. The most fatally beautiful woman stood before him. She was the kind of woman who made you want to write poetry to her. Better yet, she held out a glass toward him.

"Water?" she asked, her green eyes twinkling.

"Yes, thank you," Michael said, far too grateful to feel any embarrassment. He quaffed it greedily. He then returned the glass to the woman. "Thank you."

"You are Lord Waverly, are you not?" the woman asked.

"Yes, I am," Michael said, nodding and blinking at the same time. The woman's beauty was astounding, her air divine.

"I am Venitia Lovall," the woman said, smiling. "I've just arrived in town. I met a friend of yours, Amelia Thornton."

"Did you?" Michael asked.

"She is a very interesting and intelligent woman."

"Yes." Michael nodded, finding he was smiling widely. This woman was not only beautiful, but intelligent. Far too often people overlooked his friend Amelia's finer qualities. "She is."

"I find it strange," Venitia said with a frown, her eyes showing deep concern, "that a woman like Amelia is not engaged or married yet."

"Of course not!" Michael exclaimed.

Venitia's brow rose. "I beg your pardon."

Michael frowned in confusion. "I only meant . . . well, Amelia is a writer and artist. She—she would not be interested in things like marriage."

"But she is a woman?" Venitia asked, her eyes sparkling. "Is she not?"

"Well, yes, I suppose so," Michael said, feeling rather uncomfortable. Why he did, he could not say. "I mean, of course, she is. But marriage would end her writing career."

"Perhaps," Venitia said. Her eyes only laughed all the more. "If she married the wrong man. But writer or not, she is a woman, and a woman needs love."

"She loves her writing," Michael said, surprised at his vehemence.

"You yourself are engaged, are you not?" Venitia asked.

"Yes, yes I am," Michael said. He narrowed his eyes. "I know what you are thinking. But it is different."

"Why?"

"Because, I am a man. I will not have to forfeit my writing once I am married."

"Won't you?" Venitia asked. There was a strong amount of challenge to her words.

"No, I won't," Michael said, anger rising in him. He was rarely angry. "Estelle understands that."

"I see," Venitia murmured. It appeared she was overly interested in flicking off a speck of dust from her sleeve. "Estelle is a very beautiful woman."

Michael smiled. "Yes, isn't she? It amazes me that she chose me."

Venitia's gaze rose to his. "She chose you?"

"I-I meant that as a figure of speech," Michael said. Then a jolt shot through him. He was suddenly overcome by the need to be honest, totally honest. "No, she chose me. Sh-she proposed to me."

"She did?" Venitia asked, her gaze still compelling, almost mesmerizing.

"Yes," Michael said. "I was totally dumbfounded. Could have knocked me over with a feather. She could have her pick of any man, as beautiful as she is."

"If a man is what she wanted."

"I beg your pardon?" Michael said, offended.

"I'm sorry," Venitia said, quickly laughing. Her gaze narrowed, as if she were seeing into the very soul of him. "I did not mean to cast aspersions upon you. I only wondered if Estelle knows she has chosen a good man, for I believe you are one."

Michael flushed. "Well, I'm not sure of that. As I said, there are far better men out there."

Venitia smiled. "I don't know, but I can only hope your friend Amelia finds one just as good as you are."

Michael frowned again. "If she wishes to marry. But, as I said, she has her art. If she relinquished that . . ." He stopped and shook his head. He couldn't imagine Amelia not writing. He knew her too well. They had worked together too closely for that to happen. "No. It couldn't happen."

"Couldn't it?" Venitia murmured. She smiled. "Forgive me. I am keeping you from your fiancée. I do hope to see you again."

"Yes," Michael said. He watched as she strolled away, a frown darkening his brow. What an unusual conversation to have with a total stranger. He'd almost preferred they had talked about Prinny's jacket or some other inanity, rather than what they had discussed. It left him extremely unsettled.

He shook his head and attempted to throw off such bothersome thoughts. The woman might be beautiful, but she was completely wrong. Amelia was happy the way she was. She didn't need to marry.

"I did not know you could be so subtle," Cupid said.

"Neither did I," Venus laughed. "You are right, son. There is something challenging in doing it in this menial fashion."

"What do you intend to do now?" Cupid asked.

Venus smiled. "Why, add some healthy competition. Your Amelia and Michael are far too complacent. And complacency and love do not make good bedfellows."

"Competition?" Cupid asked with a frown.

"Yes," Venus said, her gaze narrowing. "Amelia is complacent because she doesn't have the confidence to believe she has the right to ask for anything else. She is also an innocent. She is willing to settle for what she has, because she doesn't know what love is, or what she is missing."

"And Michael?" Cupid asked, very much as one physician conferring with another.

"Oh, he is complacent, because he assumes Amelia will always be there for him and his marriage to Estelle will not interfere. He is awed he will have such a beautiful wife, when it is Amelia he should be proud to have by his side." She laughed, almost wickedly. "If he is in awe of Estelle, wait until he discovers who will compete with him for Amelia."

"Who do you intend to use?" Cupid asked.

Venus's eyes sparkled. "Those two are so very deeply mired in their complacency, I'll not depend upon another mere human."

"Then who?"

Suddenly a glowing red cloud appeared. From out of that glowing cloud a man walked. He was tall and golden, a true Adonis.

"No," Cupid groaned. "Not him."

"I'll not leave anything to chance," Venus said. "He'll be perfect."

"No, he won't be," Cupid said, his blue eyes grim. "I can't believe you chose him. I can't believe you would bring him back from the dead."

"I'm not bringing him back from the dead. I'm merely borrowing him for a while," Venus said. Her tone turned imperious. "I will win this bet."

"You must always have the grand display," Cupid muttered beneath his breath, as the man approached them. "Always overdo it."

The man halted before them. He looked to Venus. "Ah, most beautiful and fairest of goddesses, I thank you. What is your wish, I will gladly obey." He glanced at Cupid. "Hello, little man."

Cupid's lip curled. "Hello, Paris."

Chapter 2

The next morning, Amelia sat beside Michael with her paper and pen as she always did. She glanced at him, and then looked swiftly away. It seemed he was a different man this morning. A man who made her shy and nervous. She swallowed hard. Perhaps it was she who was a different woman instead, with different thoughts. And it was all Venitia Lovall's fault.

She'd spent a tormented night. Indeed, one of the most tormented nights of her life. Did she love Michael more than as her friend? How would she feel when he was married? What would she do if he no longer saw her?

Those questions, once asked, pierced her heart. Which only sent her into a spiral of confusion, for they appeared to answer the question of whether she loved Michael or not. Part of her leapt at the thought in breathless wonder, the other part shivered and wanted to find a nice, safe cave to crawl into and hide.

She quietly gazed at Michael as he wrote. She knew his every feature and look. They were dear to her, so very dear. Why had she never realized it? How did Michael feel about her? A flush, warm and embarrassed, flashed through her.

At that moment Michael glanced up. He wore a frown, an unusually dark frown. "Is something the matter?"

Amelia looked away. "No, no, of course not."

"Good," Michael said, his tone unaccountably forceful.

Amelia blinked. She looked down. "About last night . . ."

"What about last night?" Michael asked. It seemed as if he stiffened.

"I . . . well . . . you know," Amelia stammered. "Y-you know I wasn't . . . professing love to you : . . or anything."

His brow cleared. "No, of course not. I knew exactly what you meant. The others misunderstood, but you know the *ton*, they always are thinking things . . . like that."

"Yes, they . . . they do not understand that s-sometimes men and women can just be good friends." She drew in her breath. "It . . . it doesn't have to be love, does it?"

"Of course not," Michael said, laughing. It was a hearty laugh. Far too hearty for Amelia's newfound and tender emotions.

"Yes, it is funny, isn't?" Amelia said, and laughed, too, weakly. "I mean, you and me, and . . . love."

"The world does not understand us writers," Michael said. He picked up a piece of paper. Frowning, he riffled the edges and bent it. Amelia's eyes widened. He never treated his papers in such a manner. Indeed, that was a final draft of one of their poems. "But Estelle understands us, doesn't she?"

"Yes," Amelia said, her heart sinking. So much for any discussion of love between themselves. "S-she was not angry over what I did, was she?"

"No, of course not," Michael said. He appeared to be concentrating on something else. "She's a fine woman. She understands."

"Of course," Amelia said. What else could she say?

"Amelia?"

"Yes?" Amelia asked, rather fascinated and distracted. Michael was creasing the paper in half and then recreasing it!

"You . . . you never think of marriage, do you?"

"What?" Amelia asked, her gaze flying up in astonishment.

"I mean," Michael said, now cornering the paper into quarters, "you love your writing, don't you?"

Amelia flushed. "Yes, I love my writing."

"You're not like other women," Michael said, his tone firm.

Amelia blinked. "I'm not?"

"You don't think about things like . . . like marriage and all."

"No," Amelia said, striving to appear innocent. Since he hadn't even noticed she had been thinking about just those things in the past moments, she wasn't about to confess it now. "Not really."

"If you married," Michael said, amazingly folding the paper in his hands into eighths, "then you would have to stop your writing. I mean, for women, marriage is different. It's not like Estelle and me. She understands our writing. She'll never stop that."

"Sh-she won't?"

"No," Michael said. "She won't. And if you and I keep writing together, I just know we'll become published. Why, we'll be better than Byron, no doubt. We just need to keep working at it."

Amelia looked at Michael, who was now smiling happily. Rebellion, foreign and strange, reared up within her. How dare he appear so satisfied. It was not fair. Michael would be able to marry and still write with her, but she wouldn't be able to do the same. Drat it! He didn't even think she needed or wanted love or marriage. Her writing should be enough.

Her rebellion flared even higher. Why should it be enough? Faith, even Byron, great writer that he was, had love! She flushed. Well, she didn't want as much love as he had, for he had far too much, or far too many rather, but shouldn't she have some love?

"Well, that's that," Michael said, his tone cheery. He threw the now tiny ball of paper into the trash. "Let us start writing."

"Yes, that's that," Amelia said. For some reason she couldn't take her eyes from where that diminished piece of paper lay in a wad. Probably because she felt a strong kinship toward it.

"Dearest, did you do something with your hair?" Lady Thornton asked, as she and Amelia found two empty chairs at the Dearhearsts' ball and sat down. It was an even finer and grander affair than the one the night before. Lady Dearhearst and Lady Harper were strong archrivals in the social arena.

"Do you like it?" Amelia asked, her hand flying up to her curls. She had asked Simmons, her maid, if they could perhaps try something new with her hair for a change. The request had shocked Simmons to no end. In truth, it had shocked Amelia as well. However, after much effort, they had hit upon a different style.

"Yes," Lady Thornton said, nodding, "I do. It is . . . why, positively neat and orderly."

Amelia flushed with warmth. She might be nothing but a wad of paper, but at least she could have a nice hair arrangement. "Thank you."

Lady Thornton's eyes widened even more. "You are wearing your grandmother's pearls as well."

"Yes," Amelia said. "Are they too much?"

"My dear," Lady Thornton said, "one strand of pearls is certainly not too much. It's merely that I am surprised. I have begged you and begged you to wear them, and you never have. You say you will, but you always seem to forget to do so."

"I remembered this time," Amelia said, shifting uncomfortably. Her gaze traveled over to where Michael and Estelle stood. Estelle was stunning in a dress of sapphire. Diamond earrings glittered at her ears, and a diamond collar encircled her long, graceful neck. Amelia sighed. Suddenly, her pearls and new hair arrangement seemed silly. Perhaps she should just be satisfied with her writing after all.

"Oh, there is Lady Winnifer," Lady Thornton exclaimed. "She is waving at me. I wonder what she wants."

Amelia smiled. She knew very well what Lady Winnifer wanted. She was "firing off" her youngest daughter Chlorisa and would wish to talk strategy with Lady Thornton. Lady Thornton was famous amongst the matrons for her excellent matchmaking schemes. She no doubt enjoyed employing them on other women's daughters since they never succeeded with Amelia. "You certainly should go and see."

"Yes, dear," Lady Thornton said, her eyes already sparkling with missionary fervor. She rose and hastened over to Lady Winnifer. Chlorisa's romantic future would soon be assured.

Amelia sighed and glanced about her once more. Then her eyes widened, widened so far they hurt. She could have sworn she saw a red glow of some sort from across the room. She shook her head and blinked hard. Her breath wheezed from her. It wasn't a glow she had seen. Rather it was a man. He was past stunning. He was beautiful and masculine at the same time. His hair shone like the sun, and his walk was like that of an athlete, but never like any Amelia had ever seen.

He proceeded to move through the room, and clearly the other women were just as affected as Amelia. Ladies dropped their fans, their punch glasses, and their jaws as the man passed by them. Indeed, Mirabella Swanson fainted into her mother's arms.

Amelia's heart fluttered as the man continued to walk toward her. Her, mind you! He did not swerve, he did not tarry, and his fantastic gaze was upon her and her alone. Finally, he stopped before her. He did not bow. He only looked at her, his dark eyes ardent. "I saw you from across the room, and I had to come to you. I could not wait a moment more."

"Y-you couldn't?" Amelia stammered. It was amazing what a string of pearls and a new hair arrangement did after all.

"My name is Paris . . . Paris Alexandros," the man said. "I have left heaven and hell to meet you."

Amelia blinked. "Y-you have?"

"I have."

"You . . . you are not from London then?" Amelia asked, attempting to gain some form of normality. Never had any man ever talked to her in such a manner.

"No, I am from Greece," Paris said. "Though I have not lived there for ages." His eyes darkened. "I have not lived for some time . . . not until you."

"Greece?" Amelia asked. "Perhaps you know Venitia Lovall then?"

Some of the ardency left the man's eyes, and they twinkled roguishly. "I've known that goddess for quite some time."

Amelia suddenly felt much better. "Then you are friends?"

"She has championed me many times," Paris said, nodding. The musicians at that moment struck up the tune for the next country dance. Paris appeared to jump. He spun around and watched as the dancers began their first figure. His turned back to Amelia, frowning. "What are they doing?"

"Why, they are dancing."

"They are? It does not appear that way to me." He looked at Amelia, the ardency returning to his eyes. "I wish to talk to you where they do not make such sounds or move so oddly."

"You do?" Amelia asked, her heart pounding. She glanced quickly about. Women still gaped at Paris. She looked to where her mother and Lady Winnifer sat. Those two ladies appeared to be the only females in the entire room who were unaware of Paris and the stir he caused. Their heads were bent together, deep in conversation. No doubt they were far too involved in drawing up a battle plan for Chlorisa's future romance to take note of anything else.

A sudden thrill shot through Amelia. She might very well have her own romance. Why not talk to this intriguing man alone? She was not some young debutante after all. Indeed, she was quite on the shelf, so what would it matter? Besides, she had her pearls on and a new hair arrangement!

"Yes," Amelia said, rising swiftly. Feeling very adventuresome and wicked, she led Paris out of the ballroom into the hall. She noticed a delicate settee set to the side and thought to sit there. She pointed toward it and smiled at Paris, rather breathlessly. "Is this better?"

Paris shook his head, frowning. "I can still hear those sounds. Pan would disapprove. Come."

Without further discussion, he clasped up Amelia's hand. Never before having such masculine tactics employed upon her, Amelia permitted him to lead her along. "Where are we going?"

"I don't know," Paris said. He halted a moment, as if listening for something, then nodded. "I know." He led her farther through the house as if he himself was not a stranger to it. They passed two maidservants, both of whom stopped and gawked at Paris. Amelia was at first embarrassed. Then she realized, with the way they gazed at him, they most likely never even noticed she accompanied him.

"Here," Paris said, pushing wide a door.

Amelia entered, then gasped in delight. "The conservatory. However did you know?"

"I have a sense of these things," Paris said with an odd smile.

"Then you like plants?" Amelia asked, gazing about the conservatory. It was dark, lit only by the moonlight which streamed in from its floor-length windows.

"Not as much as other things," Paris said. Still holding her hand close and warmly, he led her through moon-silvered plants. It was like taking a midnight stroll through a garden, only better, since there was no February cold or snow within. They discovered a charming wrought-iron bench hidden in a cove of potted ferns and banana trees.

"We shall sit," Paris said, and did just that. Amelia, feeling suddenly shy, sat down next to him. He gazed at her one long, disconcerting moment. "You are the most beautiful woman in the world."

Amelia started. Regardless of her string of pearls and new hair arrangement, her intelligence could not swallow such a clanker. "No, I'm not. And you must know that."

Paris started back himself. He blinked his beatiful eyes. "But is that not what I am supposed to say?"

"Not when I know it is an obvious lie," Amelia said in a reasonable tone.

Paris studied her a moment, and then laughed, a clearly delighted laugh. "You must forgive me. I am accustomed to women demanding that I say it. It is a habit, as it were."

"I see." Amelia smiled. "Well, I understand that. But you need not say it with me. I know I am not beautiful, and I do not expect flattery."

He shook his head, a smile tilting his sculptured lips. "What an unusual woman you are. But I am here now. You shall be flattered."

Amelia frowned, uncertain how to take that statement. She didn't have another moment to consider it, however, for Paris immediately leaned over and kissed her directly upon the lips.

Amelia was stunned. A pleasant tingle coursed through her. Paris drew back and watched her. Bemused, Amelia placed her hands to her lips. It was her first kiss ever. "Th-that was nice."

"Nice?" Paris asked. He frowned. "Only nice?"

"Very nice," Amelia said quickly. "I meant very nice."

"I have been dead too long," Paris said, lowly. He pulled Amelia to him and kissed her once more, far more strongly and vehemently.

Michael stood by Estelle, not really paying attention to what she and Lady Farthington discussed. His gaze sought out Amelia, who sat across the room. He frowned slightly. She looked different tonight. Why she did, he couldn't determine.

Then he stiffened. A man, a man so stunning that every woman he passed gawked at him in unladylike fashion, walked up to Amelia. He spoke to her. Michael frowned severely. What the devil was the man saying to her to put such a look upon Amelia's face? Her eyes were starry, and she was flushing. Michael had never seen that look upon her face before, and he didn't like it, not one wit.

He muttered a curse when Amelia rose, and she and the man walked toward the exit doors of the ballroom.

Then they walked out of them! Michael didn't think. He bolted across the ballroom, all but mowing down anyone unfortunate enough to stand in his path. Amelia should not be alone with any man, let alone a man who looked like that!

Michael cursed doubly when he arrived in the hall. Amelia and the man were not there. He wandered down the hall, until he saw a maid. He dashed up to her. "Did you see a short, dark-haired woman pass here?"

"No," the maid said, shaking her head.

"She was with a man," Michael said. "A good-looking man . . ."

"Oh, I saw him," the maid said excitedly. "He went that way. He is the most beautiful man I've . . ."

Michael didn't wait a second but pushed past her and rushed off in the direction she had pointed. He soon came upon another maid, who was meandering along, a starry look in her eyes, like the one he had seen on Amelia's face. He stopped her. "Excuse me, have you seen a short, dark-haired woman . . . oh, never mind, have you seen a good-looking man . . ."

"The one who looked like a god," the maid murmured.

"Yes, yes, that one," Michael said impatiently.

"He went to the conservatory," she said dreamily.

"Are you sure?" Michael asked.

The maid flushed. "Yes, I . . . I could not help but watch him for . . . for a while."

"Where's the conservatory?" Michael asked.

"I will show you," the maid said eagerly. Michael permitted the maid to lead him to a door.

"It is in here," she said. "I will be glad to help you find him."

"No," Michael said grimly. "I will do that."

"Very well." The maid sighed.

Michael pushed open the door and entered. He strode

through the plants and foliage, until he heard voices. They came from a grouping of plants which formed a cove. He started toward the voices with purpose, but suddenly stumbled, even as a squawk arose from the floor. Confused, he righted himself and looked down. An inordinately large, white dove with ruffled feathers rested at his feet.

"What?" he muttered, frowning. What the devil was Dearhearst doing with a dove in his conservatory? The bird cooed and looked up at him, settling her wings. "Excuse me," he said. Then he flushed. He had actually talked to a bird!

He stepped aside to circumvent the dove, but it scurried directly into his path. He moved sharply to the other side. The dove immediately waddled under his feet again. He'd never known a dove to be so stupid. "Blast!"

Michael attempted to step over the dove. It only flapped up to a higher level, almost causing Michael to topple backward. Determination set in and Michael proceeded to take small, small steps, even while the dove fluttered madly at his feet.

"Infernal bird," Michael muttered as he finally managed, after minutes of the dodge-and-step game, to draw near enough into the cove's foliage to define voices and words.

"That was nice," he heard Amelia say.

Michael stiffened. What was nice? He pushed the branches of the bush before him aside to view Amelia sitting cozily, far too cozily, by the handsome man upon an iron bench. Her hand was to her mouth and she had that odd look upon her face again.

"Nice?" the man asked. He didn't look quite happy.

Michael felt a satisfaction, though he wasn't sure why. His satisfaction disappeared however, as he suddenly heard a flap of wings. The insane dove had flown up to his shoulder. "Shoo," Michael hissed, his focus still intent upon the scene before him.

"Very nice," Amelia said. "I meant very nice."

"Perrr, cooo," the dove said. It actually sounded like a chuckle.

"Shh," Michael said, frowning. What was not only nice, but very nice?

"I have been dead too long," the man said. He swiftly pulled Amelia into his arms and kissed her. Michael all but yelped. That was the nice they were talking about. An unknown, ugly feeling shot through him. The man wasn't as dead as he was going to be!

He started forward, but suddenly the dove dug its claws into Michael's shoulder. He bit back an enraged cry. He'd never have guessed doves possessed such sharp talons. He swatted at the bird. It only flapped its wings, smacking Michael in the face with rough feathers.

Michael, stunned that he was fighting a dove, attempted to protect himself. He grabbed desperately at the bird on his shoulder. It fluttered from his grasp and madly dipped and dived in front of his face. He lunged at it, missed the devilish bird completely, and toppled forward, crashing straight through the ferns and falling flat to the stone floor.

"Michael!" Amelia exclaimed. "What are you doing?"

Michael groaned and looked up. Amelia was still wrapped in the beautiful man's arms. At least they'd had the decency to desist kissing. "What am I doing?" He sprang up, dusting himself off in embarrassment. "Rather, what are you doing?"

"Oh," Amelia said. She had the grace to blush. "This is Paris."

"Paris? That is a city," Michael said, glaring at the man. "Why are you named after a city?"

"I'm not," Paris said, smiling. "It is Greek."

"He's a friend of Venitia Lovall," Amelia said.

"So that makes him a friend of yours?" Michael asked hotly.

"I am not a friend of hers," Paris said. "I am a worshiper of hers."

"What?" Michael asked, stunned.

Paris smiled, his gaze hot upon Amelia. "I kneel at her shrine."

"Probably so you can peek up her skirts," Michael muttered.

"Michael!" Amelia gasped, her eyes widening.

Michael stiffened. He was shocked himself that he had not only thought of such a thing, but that he'd said it. "I'm sorry. But . . . but you should not be here and doing . . . doing what you were doing."

"Why shouldn't she? She is not a married woman, is she?" Paris asked. He frowned. "You are not her husband?"

"No, I'm not," Michael said.

"Father or brother?" Paris asked.

"No, he is just a friend," Amelia said quickly.

"Good," Paris said. He gazed at her with that infernally indecent look. "I would start another war for you if need be, but there is no time."

"Thank you," Amelia said, her face confused. "I think."

"You are welcome." Paris nodded as if he were a prince or something. Michael only growled in his throat. Paris looked at him, frowning. "If you are not her husband or a relation, why do you interrupt?"

"Because, I am her friend, and I . . . I am concerned for her. Her reputation, that is," Michael said quickly. "A single woman should never be alone with a man." He glared at Amelia. "Nor should she kiss him. Especially like that!"

Paris frowned, and looked to Amelia. "I do not understand."

"Here in England," Amelia said, her face turning a bright red, "th-those are the . . . well, I'd guess you'd say the rules."

"Yes," Michael said, jerking his head in vindication.

"Truly?" Paris asked, frowning. He shook his head. "You, my lovely one, do not belong here in this place. It is cold and strange. I could show you a world . . ."

"I think you've shown her enough," Michael said, clenching his hands.

"No," Paris said. "I have not. These rules you speak of, they are not good. How can a woman ever love, if she cannot be alone with a man, or kiss him?"

"She's not supposed to love!" Michael all but shouted.

"What?" Amelia exclaimed. The embarrassed flush left her face. A definitely truculent look replaced it. "I'm not supposed to love?"

"I meant . . ." Michael began.

"No, I know very well what you meant," Amelia said. "And I don't care. Just because I'm a writer, and a woman writer, does not mean I can't love if I want to love. In fact, Venitia says one can only write well about what one knows."

"Venitia!" Michael growled. He was starting to positively loathe the woman, and he'd only met her last evening.

"Yes," Amelia said. "And I don't think I know enough about love yet. It's something which will help my writing."

Michael started back, flabbergasted. "Amelia!"

She sprang up. "In fact, I may very well become the next Lord Byron."

Paris stood as well, frowning. "Who is this Lord Byron?"

"A very well known and published poet," Amelia said, glaring at Michael. She lifted her chin. "I wish to return to the ballroom now."

"Very well," Paris said. "I do not like the sounds you call music, but for you, my beautiful one, I shall suffer it."

"Yes, let us go," Michael said stiffly.

"No," Amelia said. "I don't think you should."

"Why not?" Michael asked, frowning.

"Because," Amelia said, "you've a large rent in your jacket."

"What?" Michael looked down at himself. Half of his jacket was flapping down, torn from the shoulder. "The devil!"

"Come, Paris," Amelia said. She picked up her skirts and strode away. The Adonis fellow followed behind her like a champion.

Michael cursed. He'd have to go home. Estelle would not thank him for appearing in public in this fashion. If she hadn't liked the brown jacket, she'd certainly not like this. He suddenly heard a dove's coo overhead. It sounded suspiciously like laughter. He looked all about, but could not see the infernal bird. He'd have a talk with Dearhearst, see if he didn't. What the devil was the man doing with a dove in his conservatory?

"I'm sorry I'm late, Michael," Amelia said, dashing into the library. Normally she was never late, for she and Michael began their writing at nine o'clock sharp. This morning, she had overslept. She felt totally flustered and rather foggy-headed.

She was also forced to admit that she had tarried a little longer than usual. She wasn't quite certain what she should say to Michael. They had never really fought much over anything, unless it was in regard to the placement of words or commas or whatnot. She sighed. This was definitely not a placement-of-words issue.

Michael was already at the desk, working. He looked

up. His face was set in a definite glower. "Hello." He immediately turned his gaze back to the paper before him.

Amelia flushed as she hastened to take up her usual seat. She took her time fiddling with drawing out paper and pen and ink. Still Michael remained silent. She forced a smile. "What are we going to write today?"

"Something new," Michael said, his tone cool.

Amelia studied him. She sighed. "Michael, I am sorry."

Michael finally looked up. The tension seemed to ease from his face. "I am sorry as well."

"I . . . I know my behavior was not . . . not proper last night," Amelia said. "And I-I apologize."

"So do I," Michael said quickly, a relieved smile crossing his lips. "Only I was very concerned. It is not like you to behave . . . er, in such a manner."

"Yes," Amelia said, though she stiffened. She knew she had been utterly bold, brash, and improper, but for Michael to say it seemed rather insulting. "I think Paris . . . just overwhelmed me. You know, he said he had left heaven and hell for me."

"What?" Michael exclaimed, his face astonished.

"Yes," Amelia said. A purely feminine pride surged through her. It was ridiculous, she knew, but she still felt a twinge of pleasure.

"That's ridiculous."

Amelia flushed. "What?"

"A man can't leave both heaven and hell at the same time," Michael said. "He either leaves heaven, or he leaves hell, but he can't leave both. And not for a woman, certainly. The . . ."

Amelia sighed. "I'm sure he only meant it as a figure of speech."

"Well, it's rot," Michael said. "Poorly phrased and . . . and asinine."

"Perhaps," Amelia said, deflated.

"You must beware of the man," Michael said firmly. "If he tries to importune you again, just let me know. I'll take care of it."

"What?" Amelia asked.

Michael frowned. "He will probably attempt to see you again. After . . . well, all things considered, I am sure he will."

"Yes," Amelia said, frowning herself. "In fact he wishes to see me tonight."

Michael stared at her. "You refused him, didn't you?"

Amelia blinked. "No, of course not."

"But . . ." Michael looked confused. "I thought you said you were sorry."

"Yes," Amelia said, nodding. "I know I offended you, and said some unkind things, and for that I apologize, but I don't see why I shouldn't see Paris again."

"You don't?" Michael asked. "Amelia, surely you can't be so blind. It's as plain as a pikestaff why you shouldn't see him."

"What is?" Amelia asked.

"Why, that he is a fortune hunter."

"A fortune hunter?" Amelia's jaw definitely dropped. She and her mother were comfortably situated, but in no manner of speaking were they rich. They had connections, but no grand title. "Why ever would you think that?"

"What else can he be?" Michael retorted. "A stranger in town, he signals you out directly, speaks all that flattery and . . . and nonsense."

Amelia paled. "Why must it be nonsense?"

"Amelia," Michael said, his tone exasperated, "you are an intelligent woman. He worships at your shrine? You are the most beautiful woman?"

"Perhaps to him I am," Amelia said, anger and hurt rising swiftly in her. "And so what if he talks that way? He is a foreigner."

"And a fortune hunter," Michael said. "You are not thinking clearly."

"While you are?" Amelia asked. "I have no fortune to speak of, yet this man is after it?"

"Yes," Michael said. "And I cannot understand how you will permit yourself to be taken in by him."

"Well, I can," Amelia said, springing up. "You may not think he is sincere because he calls me beautiful when I am not, and he flatters me when . . . when I am not the type of woman men flatter, but I think he is sincere. And even if he is not," she said, flinging down her papers, "I enjoy it."

"Amelia," Michael objected, "you aren't being reasonable."

"No," Amelia said. "Love is not reasonable."

"You can't love him," Michael objected.

Amelia lifted her chin. "I may very well love him."

"You can't!" Michael said, an odd, almost feral growl coming from him.

"Don't tell me what I can and can't do," Amelia said, shaking. "I've fiddled long enough while Rome burned. I'm not fiddling anymore."

"I beg your pardon?" Michael asked, his eyes widening. "What on earth does that mean?"

"It means . . . it means that . . . I'm going now," Amelia said, attempting to keep sudden and silly tears from falling.

"Going where?" Michael asked.

"I'm going . . ." Amelia halted. Where was she going? She always wrote during the day. She drew in a deep breath. "I'm going . . . shopping."

"Shopping?" Michael asked, blinking.

"Yes," Amelia stated with renewed vigor. "I'm going t-to buy another string of pearls . . . and . . . and some new dresses. Some unreasonable, new dresses with which to attract my fortune hunter!"

"Fine, do," Michael snapped. "And I'm going to write a sonnet."

"Are you?" Amelia asked, her interest unfortunately piqued. "What kind of sonnet?"

Michael appeared taken aback. Then his face hardened. "A love sonnet, that's what I'm going to write."

Amelia clenched her fist. "Because you know so much about love?"

"Yes," Michael said angrily. "It's going to be a sonnet to Estelle for our wedding day."

Amelia stiffened as if she had been shot. If Michael had driven a knife into her heart, it couldn't have wounded her more. "I see."

Michael stared at her. A sudden, utter confusion flashed through his eyes. "Amelia, I-I don't know why I said that."

"No," Amelia said, stiffening her spine. "You love Estelle, after all. Y-you should write her a sonnet." She ducked her head and hastened to the door. "I-I hope it will be beautiful."

Chapter 3

"Well, Mother," Cupid said. "What are you going to do now?"

"This has not turned out as I intended," Venus said. She paced back and forth, though she floated above the ground a good six inches. She was clearly riled and did not waste her time with the pretense of gravity. "These ridiculous human beings! I declare, Amelia is falling in love with Paris, and Michael is following Estelle about like a puppy dog. He's falling further under her spell." She stopped. "Spell. Now . . ."

"No," Cupid said. "That is part of the bet. You can't use a love spell."

"But one simple spell would take care of this all," Venus said angrily. "I am a goddess, after all! Why shouldn't I use a spell?"

"Because," Cupid said, "every time you use a spell, the humans must love each other, even if they aren't meant to be together."

"I am Venus," Venus declared, imperiously. "I do not make mistakes."

"Romeo and Juliet," Cupid said, looking directly at her.

"Oh, very well." Venus sighed, throwing up her hands. "So they were too young. How was I to know that? Humans do strange and unusual things."

Cupid nodded. "Like killing themselves."

"To die for love is far better than to die for anything else."

"To live for love is better," Cupid returned. "Besides, Michael and Amelia aren't the type to die for love. They simply will not know true love if you don't succeed in matching them before Valentine's Day and Michael marries Estelle."

"I know," Venus said. "That much I am learning about these two."

"You should never have brought Paris into this," Cupid said. "Amelia and Michael have learned about jealousy before love."

"Paris! Do not speak to me of the man!" Venus said, throwing up her hands once more. "I have told him he can stop now. *He* says he is in love with Amelia."

"Paris is what the English call a loose fish," Cupid stated flatly. "He is in love with Amelia only because she has not succumbed to his charms so readily."

"Oh, how I'd like to . . ." Venus halted.

"Do," Cupid said. "Do whatever you wish with him."

"He does know how to tempt the gods," Venus said, her tone seething.

"Send him back," Cupid demanded. "Send him back now. He has always been trouble."

"I can't," Venus said. "He has been permitted to remain in mortal form until Valentine's eve. And if you think I am going to ask Hades to take him back to the underworld

ZEBRA HOME SUBSCRIPTION SERVICE, INC.

120 BRIGHTON ROAD

P.O. BOX 5214

CLIFTON, NEW JERSEY 07015-5214

AFFIX STAMP HERE

before that, you are wrong. Then I would owe Hades a favor, and you know how tricky he is about those things."

"Then what are you going to do?" Cupid asked.

Venus stared off into space. "It is too early, but I cannot wait. If Michael and Amelia have any passion for each other, we must divine it now."

"Passion?" Cupid asked, his tone dubious.

"I am tired of working around these two stubborn minds," Venus said. "Intelligence is a much overrated quality. Now passion, it is far less confusing."

"But . . ."

"No," Venus said. "I may have made a mistake in using Paris. But Paris's hold must be broken, or Amelia's awakening passions will be his."

"And Michael?" Cupid asked.

"His are awakening, too," Venus said. "They should not be wasted upon that Estelle creature."

"No spells?" Cupid asked.

"No spells," Venus said, sighing in exasperation. "Merely contrivance, which you so enjoy."

Cupid smiled widely. "Yes. This shall be fun."

"I am so glad you were able to come for tea," Venitia said, extending her hand to Amelia.

"Thank you." Amelia's eyes widened as she gazed at Venitia Lovall's spacious town house. Exotic was the first thought which entered her mind. Then a multitude of other words followed—Grecian, Roman, mystical.

"You are my very first guest," Venitia said, leading her to the parlor. "It seems I see so little of you these days."

"Yes," Amelia said. Once again her eyes widened. The parlor was decorated in gold, purple, and white. She sat down, staring about. Gilded cherubs and mythical creatures peeked out at her from every crook and cranny in the room's molding.

"I also do not see much of my friend Paris these days," Venitia said, laughing as she sat gracefully down upon a settee across from her.

"Y-you don't?" Amelia asked.

"He is quite enamored of you," Venitia said, her green eyes steady upon Amelia.

"Is he?" Amelia asked, flushing. In truth, she and Paris did spend an inordinate amount of time together. Which Amelia could not deny was thrilling or exciting. Never before had she ever had an ardent admirer.

"Are you enamored of him?" Venitia asked.

Amelia bit her lip. That was a question she asked herself many times. For all of Paris' wonderful declarations, for all his fervent words and kisses, something seemed to be missing. A small voice whispered inside her that it wasn't something missing, but rather someone. Someone else. Amelia shook her head to clear it. "I d-do not know."

"I see," Venitia said, smiling. "I am sure time will tell."

Thankfully, at that moment, a very, very short man entered, carrying a tea service. He wore the customary apparel of a butler, but his blue eyes twinkled so brightly and openly that he in no manner achieved the status of proper servant. He bounded across the room, his feet barely touching the carpet. He set the tray down upon the ornamental table close to Amelia. "Shall I serve the tea, my lady?"

"Of course, Cupid," Venitia said.

"Cupid?" Amelia asked.

"Yes," Venitia said. "He comes with me from my home."

"Tea, Madame," Cupid said. He lifted the gilt teapot high. Then suddenly, he lost control of it. It fell into Amelia's lap. No, to the stunned Amelia, it appeared to fly into her lap. The contents poured out upon her . . . and poured out upon her.

"Oh, dear!" Venitia cried, springing up. "Cupid, you clumsy man."

"I'm sorry, my lady," Cupid said quickly. He reached over and snatched the pot from Amelia's lap.

"Amelia, are you all right?" Venitia asked.

"Y-yes," Amelia said, blinking. She was completely drenched. How one pot of tea could have held so much liquid defied her comprehension. The tea fortunately must have been tepid, for she was not burned. Yet the most wonderful aroma arose to her. It held a different scent, an exotic, elusive scent.

"Your dress will be stained," Venitia said. "You must go and remove it. I shall have it attended to directly."

"Very well," Amelia said, feeling rather light-headed. The aroma still teased her senses.

"Cupid, do show Amelia to a room," Venitia ordered.

"Certainly, my lady," Cupid said, nodding.

"And prepare a bath for her."

"Yes, my lady."

"Oh, that won't be necessary," Amelia said, but in a mild, relaxed tone. She rose and willingly followed Cupid. He led her through the house, up the stairs, and to a door. When he opened the door, Amelia gasped, as it seemed she had been doing since she'd entered the house.

The room was large, spacious, and more of a conservatory than bedroom. Indeed, it far surpassed the Dearhearsts' conservatory, which Amelia remembered as divine. Strange, exotic plants bloomed, literally bloomed, in bright, brilliant colors. They decorated every inch of the room. Even the large bed, with four pillared columns rising from it, was twined with living vines. The sweet, drugging scent of flowers filled the air.

Amelia wandered into the room. Her eyes widened even

further when she discovered a . . . bathing pool. It certainly wasn't a tub, for it was too large, and it was formed of alabaster marble. Three maids stood, filling the pool with pitchers of water. They were quite comely, and rather than proper uniforms, they wore loose Grecian robes.

"I shall leave you," Cupid said. "The maidens . . . er maids, shall assist you."

"Thank you," Amelia said in a daze. The door shut, and the three "maids" hastened to her side.

"Thank you for coming, my lord," Venitia said, holding her hand out to Michael. "I see that you are a prompt man."

"Yes, yes I am," Michael said, clutching his manuscript in one hand and taking her hand in the other. He had attempted to steer clear of the Venitia Loveall for quite some time. He could not explain it, but he still felt as if she were at the crux of the problems between him and Amelia, whom he saw rarely these days. However, when she had written to him that she was interested in his works and thought she might know of a publisher for them, he had overcome his wariness.

"Do come into the parlor," Venitia said, walking away. Michael followed her. He noticed her taste in decor was queer and very foreign. She sat down very gracefully and motioned for him to sit upon the settee.

Just as Michael sat, her butler entered, carrying a tea tray, which he set upon the ornate table in front of the settee.

"Would you like some tea?" Venitia said.

"Yes, thank you," Michael said absently, considering more what the future conversation might hold than the matter at hand.

"Do give me your manuscript," Venitia said, reaching out.

"Certainly," Michael said. He sprang up and hastened over to render it into her hands. He returned to his seat in nervous anticipation. Amelia would be so shocked and surprised if he were able to get their poems published. Surely it would make her wish to start writing with him again rather then spending all her time with that "Foreign Fortune Hunter."

"You may pour the tea now, Cupid," Venitia said with a pleasant smile.

"Yes, my lady," the butler said. He lifted the teapot high. Then exclaiming, he dropped it. It fell in Michael's lap, its contents pouring out . . . and pouring out.

"Blast!" Michael exclaimed, jumping up in shock and fear. The teapot rolled to the floor. Fortunately Michael didn't feel burned, but he was drenched, completely drenched, and not in a dignified place. A pervasive, exotic aroma rose to his nostrils.

"Cupid!" Venitia cried. "You clumsy man! Will you never watch what you are doing?"

"I'm sorry, my lady," Cupid said, bending to retrieve the teapot.

"My lord," Venitia said. "I am dreadfully sorry. If you would like to retire to a room, I will have my maid attend to your clothing immediately."

"No . . ." Michael answered.

"I know you will not wish to appear in public in that manner," Venitia said, her tone delicate.

"No," Michael said, flushing. "No, I suppose not."

A maid suddenly appeared at the door. Or Michael assumed she was a maid, though the woman was not dressed as a proper maid, but wore light, gauzy draperies. Michael looked away in embarrassment.

"Ah, here you are," Venitia said. "Do take Lord Waverly

to a room in order that he may change. Perhaps he might like a bath as well."

"No," Michael said, shaking his head. "I'll not require a bath."'

"You might enjoy one." Venitia's eyes took on a strange twinkle. Then she looked away. "It will give me time to read your manuscript while I wait."

"Oh, in that case," Michael said, feeling far happier. No matter how dismal this scene had been, things might still work out to his benefit. He turned and willingly followed the girl, though he kept his gaze politely averted.

Cupid shook his head, looking after Michael. "This will not work, Mother."

"Why not?" Venitia asked, laughing.

"You do not know Englishmen," Cupid said. "Or Englishmen like Michael. He will not remain for one moment."

Venitia frowned. "Then you should have permitted me to use a true aphrodisiac in the tea."

"No," Cupid said, "that would not be fair."

Venitia sighed. "Have you not heard that all is fair in love and war?"

"I know," Cupid said, grinning. "You wrote the line, didn't you?"

Venitia laughed. "I did, didn't I? Well, let us go and see."

"In here, my lord," the woman said quietly in a heavy accent as she opened a door.

Michael, still attempting to keep his gaze away from the scantily clad maid, entered quickly, his eyes cast down. He heard the door close and sighed. Safe from that disconcerting view, he lifted his gaze to his surroundings. His eyes widened as an even more disconcerting scene met his gaze. He couldn't be in a bedroom! Yes, there was a bed in it, but other than that, it was a wild, exotic garden. Colors and scents assaulted him.

He stiffened when an even more disconcerting view presented itself. Or perhaps not disconcerting, but awesome. There seemed to be a large bathing pool surrounded by foliage. A woman bathed within. Her back was turned to him. All he could see was the creaminess of her shoulders and the shimmer of wet, long back hair. Nevertheless, he was mesmerized. Something in the way the woman moved at the moment, they way she turned her head, struck him. Struck him like lightning. "Amelia!" He heard a loud gasp, and the woman spun swiftly around, the water splashing loudly.

"Amelia," Michael said, this time just a whisper.

"Michael," Amelia stated, her eyes wide and alarmed.

"Amelia," Michael repeated. He could only stare. Never before had he realized how delicate and beautifully feminine were the features of her face. Or the depth and intriguing color of her eyes. Or how long and luxuriant was her hair.

"Wh-what are you doing here?" Amelia asked.

Michael couldn't help noticing she was breathing fast, for the water ebbed and rose, teasing him with the hint of smooth, rounded breasts hidden beneath. His own heart pounding, he forced his gaze to her face. "I-I came for a bath." He flushed. "I mean . . . the butler spilt . . ."

"Spilt tea on you?" Amelia asked, her eyes lighting. She gave a small laugh. "He did on me as well."

"He did?" Michael asked, smiling.

They stared at each other, almost inanely. It struck Michael how daffish he must appear, and he coughed. "Er, I—I better leave."

"No!" Amelia exclaimed.

"What?" Michael asked.

"I mean," Amelia said, an enchanting flush covering her, "I-I am finished bathing. And I am sure you will want a bath."

"But . . ." Michael said.

"*I* shall leave," Amelia said quickly. She moved toward the edge of the bathing pool. Michael couldn't help but watch her. She grabbed up a large, white bathing sheet which rested upon the side. She looked at him, her eyes shy and vulnerable. "If-if you could turn around, please."

"Oh, yes," Michael said. He spun quickly. He should leave. He knew he should, but for the life of him, he couldn't take one step toward the door. He heard splashing. He could imagine Amelia rising from the water. He swallowed hard. He heard a rustle. He imagined her wrapping the towel around her smooth, wet skin. Heat flashed through him.

Suddenly he heard a loud shriek and splash. That he couldn't imagine!

"Amelia," he cried, jerking back around in fright. He saw a flash of white in the pool. He dashed over. "Amelia!"

Amelia surfaced. She swiped at her wet hair which draped her face. "I'm, I'm all right. I-I just tripped and . . . and fell back in."

"Let me help you," Michael said, alarmed. He held out his hand. Amelia, sputtering, gave him her one hand. The other remained clutched around her sodden bath towel. Michael assisted her out of the bathing pool, automatically putting an arm about her to steady her.

"Th-thank you," Amelia said, looking up at him, her face glistening and flushed.

"You're . . ." Michael murmured. She was warm, wet, and perfect in his arms. She was beautiful, and his whole body cried out for her. He didn't finish his sentence, for there weren't any words he could speak. He wrapped his other arm around her and, bending down, kissed her.

Their lips were tentative a moment. But only a moment. Desire sublimated inexperience, and their lips melded, as if knowing each other, and needing, needing desperately. Michael's hands caressed Amelia, trembling in the delight of learning the curves and feel of her. She lifted her hands to his shoulders, only the closeness of their bodies keeping the sheet between them.

Michael groaned and shivered. Without thought, only raw need driving him, he caught Amelia up in his arms and carried her to the monstrous vine-covered bed. He laid her down, their bodies never leaving each other, as if now that they were together, they could not bear to be apart.

"I love you!" Amelia whispered.

It was spoken softly, a mere breath between impassioned kisses, yet Michael heard. The words seeped into his soul, warm and glowing. There was no explosion. No surprise. Only a pure, simple knowing. He drew back and gazed at Amelia. He loved her. He loved her completely. He slowly reached up to grasp the damp sheet between them. Amelia's eyes were warm, willing and wanting.

"Stop!" a male voice shouted.

Michael, stunned, looked up. Venitia and her butler, both of them, stood by the bed. Michael blinked. It was as if they had appeared out of thin air. Venitia was gazing at them, a look of utter astonishment upon her face. It had been her butler who had shouted. His gaze was sympathetic, but stern as their eyes met.

Reality struck Michael in that moment. He was an engaged man and he had been just about to dishonor his best friend and the woman he loved. He looked down at Amelia. She gazed up at him with dazed and loving eyes.

"Oh, God!" He rolled quickly from her, bolting from the bed. "I'm sorry, Amelia."

"No, no," Amelia said. She sat up, clutching the sheet to her. A bright red painted her cheeks. "It was . . ."

"Our fault," the butler said. "Wasn't it, my lady?"

"Yes," Venitia said. She still had a stunned look upon her face. "I had not realized that you two . . ." She shook her head. "I mean, I didn't realize until a moment ago that my silly maid had put you in the same bathing room."

"It was—" the butler began.

"An accident," Venitia finished.

"Er, yes," Michael said. He gazed at Amelia. It was an accident which now tore his soul apart. He swallowed hard. "Er . . . I'd best leave."

"Right this way," the little butler said, jumping to lead him toward the door.

Michael, with one last, longing look back at Amelia, followed him from the room in silence.

"You are still surprised, Mother?" Cupid asked, once they were alone again.

"Yes," Venitia said, frowning. "I had never expected such passion from those two. How Michael could . . . well, he certainly did not have the finesse of Marc Antony, but . . . but he had passion. And Amelia, I knew she was growing into a woman, but I . . ." She laughed. "Yes, they surprised me."

"You were brilliant when you caused her to slip," Cupid said, smiling.

"*I* did not cause her to slip," Venitia said, her brows shooting up. "I thought you had."

"No, I hadn't," Cupid said.

They stared at each other. Then they both looked upward and said not another word.

* * *

Michael sat alone in the library. He must leave soon to escort Estelle to a musical. Yet he stared at two sheets of paper on the desk. The first sheet of paper was neatly transcribed with the sonnet he had written to Estelle for Valentine's Day and their wedding. The other page was well-nigh illegible. Scribbled, with no punctuation as yet. It was a love poem to Amelia, written as swiftly and straight from the heart without thought as the moment he had bent and kissed her this afternoon.

Michael groaned. He was not a poet. He was a fool. A fool engaged to one woman and in love with another. Amelia's voice whispered once again, "I love you."

Why had he not known it before? Why had he not realized that he loved and needed her all this time? He had not been just concerned about Paris. He had been jealous. He had not missed Amelia writing with him. He had simply missed her. My God, what had he done?

Michael rose, his face grim. He was not being honorable to either. He must talk to Estelle. She was his fiancée, the one to whom he had pledged his troth, never knowing the secrets of his own heart.

"Amelia, I do not understand," Lady Thornton said, sitting upon the bed. "Why do you not wish to attend the musical this evening?"

"I-I simply do not wish to," Amelia said. She stared into her dressing-room mirror. Could her mother tell that she was a different woman? She was a woman who had recognized true love and had tasted the passion of it.

"But Paris is downstairs waiting to escort you," Lady Thornton said. "You and he did not have a disagreement did you?"

"No." Amelia sighed. She could not say it was only the disagreement of her heart which stopped her. She could not say she was not prepared to see Michael this evening, not after this afternoon. She had declared her love for him and would have willingly given her body and soul to him. He had said he was sorry and left.

"Then why . . ." Lady Thornton said.

"Mother," Amelia said, her voice crisp and tense, "please, do not ask questions. I-I will go downstairs and explain it to Paris."

She rose. Was she being a fool? Paris proclaimed his love to her every day. He flattered her and made her feel wonderful about herself. Indeed, it was he who had given her a confidence she had never possessed before.

Yet in all good conscience, she could no longer accept his vows of love. Not when her heart vowed itself to another. Nor could she accept his kisses anymore. Not when her lips only desired Michael's and her body demanded his touch and only his.

"Lady Carstair, could I please have a word with Estelle in private?" Michael asked as he entered the Carstair's town house. "It . . . it is important."

"I don't know," Lady Carstair said, looking hesitant.

"Mother, we *are* engaged," Estelle said, her tone cool.

"Very well," Lady Carstair said. "For a few minutes. Then we must hurry so we are not late for the musical."

"Come, Michael," Estelle said. Turning, she led him into the drawing room. She took a seat and looked at Michael in inquiry.

Michael found he could not sit. He paced over to the fireplace, unable to look at her. "Estelle, why do you wish to marry me?"

"What?" Estelle asked.

"Why did you choose me?" Michael asked. "Out of all the men you could have married, why did you choose me?"

"What an unusual question to ask," Estelle said, appearing surprised.

"No," Michael said. "We shall be married within the week, and I wish to know."

Estelle shrugged. "I chose you because I believe we are a very suitable match. Your fortune is comparable to mine, your title is indeed better than mine, and I believe we are very compatible."

"Why do you think we are compatible?" Michael asked. "I am absentminded. I am a poet. You must even tell my servants what I should wear and when I should wear it."

Estelle nodded. "Yes, and I like that."

"You do?" Michael asked.

"Yes," Estelle nodded. "Most men are contrary and difficult. They never listen to one. You are not that way. You listen and obey me. Nor do you cling to my skirts, or demand . . ." She stopped all of a sudden.

Michael frowned. "Demand what . . . ?"

"Nothing," Estelle said.

"Demand what?" Michael asked again. For the first time ever he saw Estelle flush. Then it struck him. He knew. He knew for he now understood how passion could demand passion. Good Lord in heaven. He had never tried to kiss Estelle. Why hadn't he? "You mean I have never demanded anything physical from you."

"Yes," Estelle said, looking him fully in the eye.

"I see," Michael said, feeling as if she'd punched him in the stomach.

"I do not care for such," Estelle said. "All that pawing and mauling."

"Wh-what did you think would happen once we were married," Michael asked, amazed. "Did you think we would not have children?"

"Of course we will have children," Estelle said. Her face shaded slightly, almost in disgust. "I promise you, I shall do my duty by you. I want children."

"Your duty," Michael wheezed. He stiffened. "Then you do not love me?"

"Love?" Estelle asked. She stared at him. "Of course not. Love is for—for the commoner. It has nothing to do with those of our position."

Sudden ire sparked in Michael. "I believe in love. Why wouldn't you think I believed in love?"

Estelle blinked. "We have never discussed it, I assume."

Michael paled. He'd been so busy in his own world, that in truth, they *had* never discussed it. Or anything else, for that matter. He'd just been so stunned that she had proposed to him that he had assumed she loved him. "I see."

Estelle's gaze turned cold. "You are only experiencing wedding nerves. Mother says all men experience it. Father did, and if Mother hadn't held firm, I'm sure I wouldn't be alive today."

Michael laughed. "Are you alive?"

"What does that mean?" Estelle asked.

"Nothing," Michael said. How could he insult her, when it was he himself who had been just as bad as she. He flushed. "Then you truly believe we will have a good marriage."

"We will," Estelle said, her tone firm. "With your fortune and mine, and your title, we shall gain rank and position swiftly. Once you take up your seat in the House, we shall rise in fame and power."

Michael stared, shocked. "But I am no politician."

"You do not have to be," Estelle said, her eyes finally glowing with fervor. "Not with me by your side. I shall see to it."

Michael shook his head. "No, I am a writer and poet."

Estelle looked at him and then looked away swiftly. Yet not swiftly enough. Michael had seen it in her eyes. He sucked in his breath. "You don't believe that. Y-you don't want me to be a writer."

She laughed and waved a negligent hand. "I am sure you enjoy that now, but you will change. One of these days scribbling away with Amelia will not be enough."

"You mean not enough for you," Michael said.

Estelle rose, the first sparks of anger flaring in her eyes. "Yes, not enough for me."

Michael saw his future before him. "Estelle, release me."

Estelle stiffened. "No, I shall not. As I said, you are experiencing nothing but nerves. They will pass. I will not permit you to destroy our future because you are suddenly turning weak and craven."

"I love Amelia," Michael said softly.

Estelle blinked. Nothing more. "Yes?"

"Don't you understand," Michael said, his voice rising. "I love Amelia."

Estelle's eyes remained stern. "I told you, I do not believe in love. If you must suffer such low emotions, then I'd as soon they were bent upon Amelia. As long as you are discreet, I will not object. But you have pledged your troth to me, and I will not release you."

"Estelle . . ." Michael said.

"No," Estelle said, her tone firm. "We have been engaged for six months, and at no time have we had these disagreements before. I do not believe they mean anything. I will not permit you to destroy my plans."

"Your plans!" Michael exclaimed.

Estelle looked at him sternly. "You are a man of honor, I believe? Now come, we will be late for the musical."

Without another word, she turned and swept from the room. Michael stared after her, his heart chilling. He was a man of honor. Numbly, he followed her.

* * *

"Amelia," Paris said, standing as she entered the parlor. He rushed over and grasped up her hands, kissing them. "You are beautiful, as always."

Amelia flushed. "H-hello, Paris."

"We shall go to hear more of your English music," Paris said, smiling. "See, I learn and accept. But someday, when you hear my music, you will know what music is."

"I-I do not feel like going to the musical tonight," Amelia said.

"You do not?" Paris asked, frowning. "Then what is your wish, my divine woman."

"I-I do not wish to do anything tonight," Amelia said, quickly pulling her hands from his and scurrying away.

"You do not, my love?" Paris asked.

"Please, do not call me your love," Amelia said, choking.

"But you are my love," Paris said, his eyes darkening. "I worship at your feet, I . . . yes, I adore you."

"Paris," Amelia said, drawing in her breath and finally looking at him, "I-I must tell you something."

"Tell me," Paris said. "Tell me anything."

"I-I am in love with Michael," Amelia said. She expelled her breath. There, she had said it.

"What?" Paris looked totally flabbergasted, a very odd look upon such a beautiful man.

"I love Michael."

"You love Michael?" he repeated, as if he still could not understand.

"Yes, I love Michael."

"But you cannot," Paris said, his voice rising. "I am here."

It was Amelia's turn to stare. He has said it simply, with complete confidence. A nervous laugh escaped her. She flushed then, in embarrassment. "I'm sorry, Paris, but I love Michael."

"I do not understand," Paris said, frowning. "Am I not more handsome?"

"Yes," Amelia admitted. "You are more handsome. Though I think Michael very good-looking."

"He is not . . . he does not charm you?" Paris asked, his face darkening even more.

"No, he does not flatter me," Amelia returned. "But, yes, he charms me in many, many ways."

"I am stronger than Michael!"

"Yes, you are stronger."

"I have been a prince in my time!"

Amelia blinked. "You have?"

"Yes," Paris said, glaring at her.

Amelia shrugged helplessly. "Then you are a prince."

"And I know the gods," Paris said, growing even more wroth. "Your Michael, he has never had the gods talk to him, has he? They have never championed him?"

"No, I don't think so," Amelia said, feeling totally out of her depth.

"Then why do you love him rather than me?" Paris asked. He almost jumped up and down in anger, very much like a spoiled schoolboy.

"Because I do," Amelia said, her own ire rising. "Michael may not be as handsome as you, or as strong, or . . . or anything else, but I love him. I have always loved him."

"No," Paris said, shaking his head. "This is *her* work. You cannot love that common, ordinary man."

"Michael is not common and ordinary," Amelia said angrily. She frowned. "Whose work?"

"You are under a spell," Paris said. "You must be."

"That is ridiculous," Amelia snapped. "It is no spell. I simply love Michael."

"No," Paris said. "You do not. You must love me. I shall see to this."

With that, he turned and strode from the room. Amelia blinked. She was a novice at rejecting a man, but the manner in which the scene had ended seemed queer, very queer indeed.

"Venus!" Paris shouted, bursting into the town house. It was uncommon that he had been forced to go to a literal address, but he had called her and called her, and she had not appeared. "Venus!" he shouted once more, charging through the house, searching the rooms. He halted when he looked into the parlor.

Venus and Cupid were sitting, drinking from teacups.

"Hello, Paris," Venus said, holding her cup up. "Do join us. It is teatime."

"Teatime?" Paris asked, frowning.

Venus laughed. "When in Rome, do as the Romans do."

"Why have you not come to me?" Paris demanded, stalking into the room.

"Because you are throwing one of your tantrums," Venus said with a shrug. "I do not wish to deal with it at the moment. I far prefer tea."

"I'll pour you a cup, Paris," Cupid offered, his blue eyes twinkling.

Paris stiffened. "I don't want that disgusting mixture. I want to know what you did to Amelia."

"I didn't do anything," Venus said.

"You put a spell on her, didn't you?" Paris asked.

"No, I didn't," Venus said.

He glared at Cupid. "Then you! You shot her with an arrow."

"You know he didn't, Paris," Venus said, her tone exasperated. "And you know I didn't. That was the whole purpose of this little bet, one which I am glad to say, looks like I will win."

"No," Paris said angrily. "Amelia cannot love Michael. She must love me."

"She does love him," Venus said. "I have cast no spell. Why, my interventions have been small, minimal. She loves him all on her own, Paris."

"She can't love him," Paris said. "I want her. You must help me!"

Venus's eyes turned cold. "No, I will not. I helped you once, and it caused an entire war. At the time, I found it amusing, and you amusing, but I do not any longer."

"You must help me," Paris repeated, more in anger than in request.

"No," Venus said. "You only want Amelia because you cannot have her."

"No," Paris said, shaking his head. "I love her. She is different than any woman I have ever met."

"Of course she is different," Cupid said. "She is English and not of your time."

"No," Paris said. "It is more than that, and I want her."

"Why?" Venus asked, her eyes narrowing. "You will not be here beyond a few more days. If you love her, then you will let her go. She is of the living, and she loves another man. If you love her, then you will accept this."

Paris stared. "I want her, Venus. Help me."

"No," Venus said firmly. "Not this time."

"You will be sorry," Paris warned, slowly backing away. He turned and ran from the room.

Cupid frowned. "He bears watching."

"No." Venus laughed. "Paris is harmless. He was nothing without me, and will be nothing. Let him pout and stew. Let him try and gain Amelia's love without me. He will fail."

"Very well," Cupid said. "But what are we going to

do with Estelle? Now her, I would not mind turning into stone."

"No," Venus said. "I will take care of her in my time. How dare she deny love. Or call it common. Even the gods cannot deny it without my vengeance upon them. But I'll not use my powers as yet. I am going to win this bet of yours, my son. Win it . . . fair and square, as they say here in this England."

Chapter 4

"Hello, Amelia," Michael said, looking up from his desk. His heart beat faster, even as pain flashed through him. He had not seen her at the musical the night before. He'd thought it was a blessing at first, but then a fear had taken hold she might not come to write this morning. He knew he had to see her. "I did not see you at the musical last night."

"No," Amelia said, not meeting his gaze. "I . . . I did not . . ." She didn't finish her sentence but walked over to take up her place beside him.

Michael drew in a breath. She was so near. He remembered yesterday, holding her and kissing her. He groaned. How many times had they sat together like this, without him ever knowing how she felt in his arms, ever knowing he loved her? How many moments he had lost and would never have now.

He glanced at her. She would not look at him. He coughed, knowing what he must do. "I-I must apologize for yesterday." Her eyes flew to his, stunned and hurt. He clenched his fist.

He was a man of honor. To speak of love to Amelia would be wrong. He was an engaged man. Estelle would not release him. "I-I don't know what happened to me."

"I-I understand," Amelia said. Her smile was so obviously forced Michael wanted to reach out and hold her. "I-I don't know what happened either. It must have been . . ."

"The place," Michael said quickly.

"Yes," Amelia said just as quickly.

"And . . . and well, the situation," Michael said.

Amelia nodded. "Yes. I don't know how . . . how that happened."

"They are rather odd," Michael said. "I mean, Venitia Lovall and her butler . . ."

Amelia giggled. "Especially the butler. I've never seen such a clumsy man before. To drop a pot of tea on two people in the same day!"

Michael laughed. "It had to be almost within minutes of each other."

"Only imagine," Amelia said. The laughter died from her eyes, and she fell silent.

"Well," Michael said, forcing a jovial tone, "we should not feel bad . . . I mean guilty because of what happened."

"I do not feel guilty," Amelia said, looking him directly in the eye.

Michael tensed. He couldn't say he didn't feel guilty. He did. Guilty for not knowing he loved Amelia until it was too late. Guilty for promising himself to another woman when it should have been Amelia. "Good. Then this . . . this won't ruin . . . ruin our . . . er, working together, or anything. We are friends?"

"Yes," Amelia said, her voice almost a whisper. "We are friends."

Michael forced a smile. "Then let us start working. You know, Venitia says she might have a publisher interested in our work. We really should revise that last poem."

"Yes," Amelia said. "We should."

"Just friends?" Venus asked, laughing.

"You are not upset?" Cupid asked, frowning.

"No," Venus said. She shrugged. "Let them suffer denied love for a while, if they wish to do so. Michael is merely being a typical man. They are so much slower than women."

"But the wedding will be within the week."

Venus chuckled. "Oh, he will confess his love by then."

"You are positive?"

"If he doesn't," Venus said, a smug smile upon her lips, "I will assist him. But not until then. Let him learn the pains of denying love. He will respect it all the more, once he confesses it and knows the sweetness of it."

Amelia entered the library. Michael was not there. She didn't wonder. It was the day before his wedding. She had expected they would not work today, but he had been almost adamant that they should.

Her heart twisted. She thought she would die, working with Michael every day and loving him as she did, knowing he did not love her. Then she would think about not seeing him at all, and it seemed worse. Every night she thought she could not tolerate it, that she must say good-bye to him and start another life. And every morning, she would wake up, knowing she must see him. She would take whatever moments she had with him.

She walked over to the desk and sat down in his chair.

She wanted to glance over once again the poem they had been working on for Venitia Lovall's publisher. The poem lay squarely in the middle of the desk. She picked up the paper to study it.

Her eyes widened. It was not the poem they had been working upon before. Rather it was a far different poem. It had been scribbled, and the punctuation was atrocious, but Amelia read it, every scrawled word finding a home within her soul. She promptly burst into tears, clutching the paper to her heart.

"Amelia," Michael's voice exclaimed from the door. "What is the matter?"

Amelia looked up, barely able to see him through her tears. "I . . . I . . ." She shook her head, unable to speak. "It . . . it is beautiful."

"What is beautiful?" Michael asked, rushing over to her and kneeling down.

"Your poem t-to me," Amelia sobbed.

Michael stiffened. "H-how did you find that?"

"It . . . it was on the desk when I came in," Amelia sobbed.

"On the desk?" Michael asked, paling.

Amelia nodded. "I-I thought y-you didn't love me."

Michael remained frozen a moment. Then his face twisted. "I do love you, Amelia. God help me, but I do!"

"Oh, Michael!" Amelia cried.

He reached out for her at the same time she held out her arms. The leather chair squeaked and was shoved rudely away as their bodies came together. They toppled to the ground, their lips meeting in a kiss which was savage from need too long denied.

"You love me," Amelia whispered, wildly kissing Michael's cheek, his eyes, his forehead. "You love me!"

"Yes, Amelia," Michael said hoarsely. "My lovely Amelia!"

Their bodies entwined and their hands sought and caressed each other in fevered desire. Amelia, with no thought, only need, shoved at Michael's jacket. It was a hated barrier to her love. Michael reached to snatch at the buttons at Amelia's throat. The first one snapped off and flew. Amelia only laughed.

Michael didn't. He froze, his face full of consternation. "Oh God! What am I doing?"

"What?" Amelia asked. She shook her head. "It doesn't matter."

"I can't do this," Michael said, his voice rough. He tore himself from Amelia's arms, and stood. Stunned and chilled with the shock of abandonment, Amelia slowly sat up.

Michael refused to look at her. "I'm sorry, Amelia."

"Sorry?"

He groaned. "I . . . I never meant t-to tell you, never meant to . . . to kiss you."

Amelia paled. "You didn't?"

"I must marry Estelle," Michael said, his voice tormented. "She . . . she will not release me."

"You asked?" Amelia said, her heart wrenching both in love and pain.

"Yes. She says she will hold me to my vow, and . . . and to my honor."

"I see," Amelia said. She rose slowly, a blessed numbness overtaking her.

Michael looked at her then, stark agony within his eyes. "I'm sorry, Amelia."

"No," Amelia said, shaking her head. "I-I understand. Y-you cannot withdraw, it is too late."

"Yes," Michael said. "Too late."

They gazed at each other for a long, desperate moment. Amelia forced a smile. "I-I think I'd best leave now."

Michael's eyes turned pleading. "I-I will see you at the wedding tomorrow?"

"Yes, you will see me at the wedding," Amelia said.

She knew she lied.

"What? What are they doing?" Venus asked, her green eyes a mix of surprise and anger. "They should have made love. He should have proposed!"

"It is honor, Mother," Cupid said, sighing heavily. "Here in England it is the most important thing, above all else."

"Don't speak to me of honor," Venitia snapped, anger all but crackling from her. "Mankind has often erred and chosen honor over love. I have a good mind to . . . to turn them both into something. Statues to the shrine of Athena! All intellect and nothing more."

"No," Cupid said quickly. "Do not lose your temper, Mother!"

"Not lose my temper!" Venus snarled. Her eyes shot fire. "I have wasted my time upon these two imbeciles. I have brought them to their rightful love. I have shown them their passion, and yet they will turn away for some such notion as honor?"

"They need your help," Cupid said, his tone coaxing.

"I will help them," Venus said, her eyes narrowing in a look Cupid knew all too well. It was her look before women turned into trees and men into odd combinations of beast and man. "I will . . ."

"No," Cupid exclaimed. "There is still tomorrow. Michael and Amelia might still have a chance. Why not wait and see what they do first?"

Venus glared at him, though some of the wrath gratefully drained from her eyes. "Very well. But if they remain the mortal fools they are, and I lose this bet, I will . . ."

"There is a feast at Olympia tonight," Cupid said quickly. "You should go to it. Then see how you feel tomorrow."

Venus studied him one long moment. Then she shrugged. "I shall return in the morning." She disappeared in a glimmer of light.

Cupid sighed in relief. That had been a very close call. His mother was infamous when she lost her temper.

Amelia sat silently in the parlor. Her mother, after pleading and begging, had finally left for the wedding without her. She blinked back tears. Surely she had cried them all out already. Her chest tightened in panic. What was she going to do? She knew she would never have the strength to see Michael day after day, knowing they must both deny their love. She remembered the agony in his eyes when he had told her he was sorry. She could not bear it, as much for him as for herself.

Her butler entered at that moment, and Amelia immediately forced a smile. "Excuse me, Miss Amelia, but Mr. Alexandros has arrived and wishes to speak to you. I told him you were not receiving, but he says he must speak with you."

"Oh," Amelia said. She sighed. "Then I shall see him."

"But Miss Amelia . . ." her butler said.

"I will see him," Amelia said more firmly.

"Very well, miss," her butler said. His face showed clear disapproval as he turned and left.

Amelia sighed again. It didn't matter to her anymore. Nothing did.

Within seconds, Paris rushed into the parlor. His arms were outstretched. "My love!"

Amelia gazed at him, this beautiful man with the open

arms, and immediately burst into tears. How cruel fate was. "I'm not y-your love!"

"Yes, you are," Paris said. He crossed to her and sat, enfolding her. Amelia was crying too much to object. "You are my love."

"N-no," Amelia sobbed on his shoulder.

Paris only held her all the tighter. "Come away with me, Amelia. Please, come away with me."

Amelia choked on a sob. "What?"

"Come away with me," Paris repeated. "Michael marries today. He does not love you."

"Yes, he does," Amelia said. "But . . . but he is honor-bound."

"Honor-bound?" Paris asked. He blinked, as if the concept was foreign to him. Then another light entered his eyes. "Then there is nothing else you can do. He can give you nothing. While I, I can give you everything. I can show you a world you have never seen, Amelia. And I will worship you always."

"Are you insane?" Amelia asked.

"Insane with want of you," Paris said, vehemently. "Come with me."

Amelia stared at Paris. Suddenly it was she who felt insane. She could not remain here. She would be living in perpetual misery. Michael would be living in perpetual misery. She must have the strength to end it for them both. If it took putting a world between them, then she would do it.

"Come with me," Paris said again.

"Yes," Amelia agreed, almost with a relieved sigh. She was tired, so very tired. "Let us go."

"My coach awaits," Paris said, rising. "Come, my love."

"But shouldn't I pack?" Amelia asked, standing as well.

"No," Paris said. "You need not take anything with you where we are going."

"What?" Amelia asked, blinking.

Paris flushed. "I mean . . . we will get you new clothes, my beautiful one. All the clothes you could ever dream of. But only come with me now."

"Yes." Amelia sighed. She went and picked up her reticule. It truly was better this way. She didn't need time to think. Paris was taking care of everything.

"Mother!" Cupid's voice exclaimed before he even materialized into the middle of Venus' bedroom on Mount Olympus.

"Hmm," Venus murmured, from her divine bed and bower.

"You must come fast," Cupid said.

Venus opened her eyes, which were bleary. She had definitely drunk too much ambrosia punch last night. "What?"

"Paris has done it again," Cupid said, his tone exasperated.

"Done what again?" Venus murmured, slowly sitting up.

"He's stolen Amelia and run away with her!"

"What?" Venus asked, frowning. "Why would she do a thing like that?"

"For love, Mother," Cupid said. "Are you pleased, now?"

"No," Venus said, spring from her bed.

"I told you we must watch him," Cupid said. "You should never have brought him back into the world."

"But he has only today," Venus cried. "Why would he try and run away with Amelia now?"

"That is what I want to know," Cupid said. "And something tells me it is not good. Do hurry."

"Indeed," Venus said. She raised her arms. "We shall go to him, now!"

* * *

The coach traveled along at a fast pace. Amelia lay fast asleep upon the seat. Paris sat quietly upon the other, gazing at her. Suddenly there was a rush of wind, a glimmer of light, and Venus and Cupid sat upon both sides of Amelia.

"What are you doing, Paris?" Venus asked without preamble.

"Hello, my most beloved goddess," Paris said, smiling. "I expected you before this."

"Well," Venus said, her tone cranky, "there was a feast at Olympus last night."

"Amelia," Cupid said. "Wake up."

"She can't hear you," Paris said, smiling.

"Why, what have you done?" Cupid asked.

Paris laughed. "It is not what I have done. But rather, what Hades has done."

"Hades?" Venus asked, narrowing her yes. "What has he to do with this?"

"Since you denied me your help," Paris said, his beautiful face turning cold, "I went to him for assistance."

"What kind of assistance?" Venus asked.

Paris smiled. "There are so very few new souls in the underworld these days. Not since the belief in it has, pardon the expression, died out." He shrugged. "They all choose to go to Heaven or Hell now. So it gets lonely in the underworld. Or dull, rather. Amelia will be a welcome addition."

"No," Venus said. "Hades cannot do this."

"He can if Amelia chooses to cross the river with me," Paris said. He smiled smugly. "You know the rules. Or do you wish to go down to the underworld and argue with Hades?"

Venus cringed. "You know I will not."

"Even Zeus does not tangle with Hades," Cupid said angrily.

"No," Paris said, laughing.

"Amelia!" Venus said, gazing at the sleeping girl with a fire in her eyes. Light shimmered and flared about them. Still Amelia did not awaken.

"I told you," Paris said. "She will not hear you or see you. Hades holds her in the dreamworld. She is out of your sanction, as it were."

"Out of my sanction!" Venus all but shouted.

Paris's eyes darkened. "You have played your games with Amelia, why cannot Hades? He is only making sure Amelia has the right to make her own decision."

"But with lies and deceit," Cupid exclaimed.

Paris shrugged. "It is not uncommon for any of your family, is it?"

"You said you loved Amelia," Venus said, her eyes narrowing. "How can you take her life like this?"

"I will give her a better life," Paris said. "Far better than what Michael can give her. I will give her eternity, with the help of Hades, that is."

"I have championed you always," Venus exclaimed. "How can you repay me like this?"

Paris's face darkened. "For every gift you have given me, there has been pain as well."

"That is love," Venus said, angrily. "That is life. The soul does not grow without both light and dark."

"You forget," Paris said with a laugh. "My soul has not been living for quite a while. Do not think to talk me out of this, my beautiful goddess." His eyes narrowed. "Nor to talk Amelia out of it. Hades wants a new soul, and I want Amelia."

"We waste time here, Mother," Cupid said.

Venus glared at her son, and then a slow smile crossed

her lips. "Yes, we do." She looked at Paris. "For all the gifts I have given you, you have never learned. But do not underestimate love. Farewell for now, my spoilt boy."

Venus and Cupid, with an understanding glance at each other, disappeared from the coach.

"At least I hope he underestimates it," Venus said lowly as both she and Cupid appeared within St. Peter's Church. Wedding guests filled every pew. Michael and Estelle stood at the altar. The minister was saying, "Speak now or forever hold your peace . . ."

"We are in time," Cupid said, grinning.

"What?" Venus asked.

"I know this part," Cupid said. "The English are forever practical. The minister is asking if anyone objects."

"Indeed?" Venus asked. "What an odd people. In Greece that would definitely be an invitation for war. But when in England . . ." She transported herself to directly behind Michael and Estelle, showing her true divinity to all. "I object!"

The wedding guests shrieked and gasped. The maids of honor either fainted or tossed up their flowers.

"So do I!" Cupid said, appearing not one second behind her.

The minister dropped his Bible. "Oh God! Oh God!"

Estelle spun around, all but entangling herself in the train of her wedding gown. Since she had not seen their form of arrival, she only glared at Venus and Cupid in undisguised anger. "What?"

Michael turned as well. His eyes widened. "Venitia!"

"Michael, who are these people?" Estelle asked, her voice rising to a loud pitch, while every other mortal in the church had grown wisely silent. "Why are they interrupting our wedding?"

"It's Venitia Lovall," Michael said, his eyes wide in confusion. "And . . . her butler."

"Her butler?" Estelle asked, her face turning dark. "A *butler* dares to interrupt my wedding?"

"Michael, you must save Amelia," Venus said, ignoring Estelle and gazing directly at him.

"What?" Michael asked. "What has happened to Amelia?"

"Paris has stolen her," Venus said.

"That . . . that blighter!" Michael exclaimed.

"She went with him because her heart was broken," Cupid said, his eyes dark. "She could not remain, knowing she and you must deny your love."

"My God," Michael said, turning pale. "Where are they?"

"We will tell you later," Cupid said quickly before Venus could speak. "But you must come with us now. It is a matter of life and death. We are powerless with Amelia for the moment, but you as a mortal still have your own will and fate."

"Then I will come," Michael said.

"Michael," Estelle stated, her tone one of command. "You cannot leave now. You can attend to Amelia after the ceremony."

"It will be too late by then," Cupid said. "Far too late!"

"You will not dare to leave me," Estelle warned, bending an even sterner look upon Michael.

"You must choose, Michael," Venus said. She jerked her head toward Estelle. "Either that creature or Amelia."

"Creature?" Estelle screeched. "Creature!"

"I will come with you," Michael said quickly. He looked to Estelle. "I am sorry, Estelle."

Estelle reached out, clutching his arm. "No! You have given your troth to me. I will sue you for breach of promise."

"Then sue me," Michael said, his voice firm.

"We must go," Venus said. She looked Michael directly in the eyes. "I warn you now. If you love Amelia, you must be prepared to accept and face things you have never ever imagined or believed."

Michael met her look, his own unflinching. "To save Amelia, I will face anything."

"Very well," Venus said.

"No!" Estelle cried, still clutching tightly to Michael. "You will not ruin my wedding day! You will not ruin my plans!"

Venus glared at Estelle, her eyes taking on that *particular* look. "Choose to release him now, or I will take you with us. Indeed, it will be all my pleasure, I assure you."

Estelle's chin lifted. "I'll not release him."

"Very well," Venus said.

"Mother!" Cupid objected. But it was too late in the shimmer and light.

"Where are we?" Estelle screamed, as all four suddenly appeared in a strange place. They stood outside a cave. The landscape was anything but English.

"We stand outside the cave to the underworld," Cupid said, his voice solemn.

"Who are you?" Michael asked, peering at Cupid in shock.

"I am Cupid," Cupid said. "And this is Venus."

"My God," Michael gazed. "I don't believe it!"

"There is no time to believe or disbelieve," Venus said quickly. "Amelia is in there. Paris wishes to take her to the underworld."

"What is the underworld?" Estelle asked, frowning.

"It is . . . it is the land of the dead in Greek and Roman mythology," Michael said.

"It's not a myth," Venus said.

"Both heaven and hell," Michael murmured. He stiffened. "How could I have been so blind?"

"What are you talking about?" Estelle asked sharply. She glared at Cupid and Venus. "You have ruined my wedding day."

"You must stop Amelia," Venus said. "If you love her, you must stop her from crossing the river. Hades wants her, and so does Paris."

"God," Michael said.

"He is not in our circle," Venus said. "But if you want His help, please do ask. You'll need it, for Cupid and I cannot, or will not, enter the cave."

"Yes," Michael said, nodding. He moved directly toward the entrance.

"Where are you going?" Estelle asked.

"To save Amelia," Michael said over his shoulder.

"This is ridiculous!" Estelle shouted, and stamped her foot.

"I don't care," Michael called. "I love her."

He disappeared into the mouth of the cave.

"Michael, stop this instant!" Estelle cried. She picked up her skirts and dashed after him. "You will listen to me!"

"Mother!" Cupid exclaimed. "Stop her!"

"No," Venus said, smiling wickedly. "Hades shall have his soul after all and Paris that woman for eternity!" She waved her hand and a stream of light streaked toward the departing Estelle. It flared and appeared to bounce off of her. Venus whipped her hand back, a stunned look upon her face. "Great Zeus!"

* * *

"Amelia, wake up." Paris's voice intruded upon Amelia's dreams. They were drugging, formless dreams, a dark elusive shadow hidden in the mist.

Amelia started and opened her eyes. She blinked, feeling an utter relief in being awake. "What? Where are we?"

"We are here," Paris said.

"Here?" Amelia peered out the window of the coach. The weather must have turned extremely foul while she had slept, for it was quite overcast outside. "Where is here?"

"Come," was all Paris said. He opened the door and alighted. He held out his hand, and Amelia, still blinking away her confusion, tumbled out of the coach.

Then she shook her head all the more. She didn't recognize the landscape whatsoever. Just how long and how far had they traveled? A grassy slope ran down to a murky, slow-running river, one she could not see across. The water certainly looked dirty enough to be the Thames, but there was no bridge, and no London. "Where are we? Is this part of the Thames?"

"The Thames?" Paris asked. Then he smiled. "Yes, yes it is. Only it is a . . . different part."

"Oh," Amelia said. An extreme unease filled her, but she refrained from comment. Having lived in London all her life, she told herself she should be prepared for new things. She was leaving her world behind after all. She was leaving Michael behind. Her heart wrenched, but she plucked up her courage. "Very well."

"Walk with me down to the river," Paris said. He took up her hand and led her to the water's edge. Amelia shivered for some reason, feeling a sudden sense of unreality.

The land and the river remained quiet, almost too quiet. Amelia had the oddest feeling of seeing, but not seeing, things.

She looked out across the river. "Are we going to cross it?"

"Yes," Paris said.

"Where is the bridge?"

"There isn't one here," Paris said. "We must wait for the ferryman." He pointed. "Here he comes."

Amelia gazed out across the river. A rickety boat, with one sole man, using a long pole, appeared. Amelia was amazed. Either the pole must be extremely long for such depths, or else there was no current. In either event, the ferryman soon transversed the river and ran the aged craft up to shore.

"You are late," Paris said to the ferryman, who was small and wizened.

The man cackled. "Don't be rushing the lady's fate any faster than yer ought, just because yers is set, jackanapes."

"Jackanapes?" Paris exclaimed, blinking.

The old man winked. "Oi've studied up on this, just like—well, you knows who wanted me ter do. I kinder likes it, s'truth."

"I see," Paris said, nodding.

The old man looked at Amelia. "Well, missy, are ye ready fer this here ferry ride?"

"I-I think so," Amelia said, her heart failing her.

"No." The old man shook his head. "You got ter be sure like. Ain't taken ye across, unless ye say you wants ter go, for I won't be bringing you back."

"Say yes, Amelia," Paris said, his tone urgent. "Please, say yes."

"And I wants her coin," the ferry man said.

"I beg yer pardon?" Amelia asked, stunned.

"Ye got to give me coin," the ferryman said. "Or you ain't going across."

"I'll pay for her," Paris said quickly.

The old man chucked. "You are hoity-toity, Prince, but there are some rules that ain't going ter change, even fer you. The lady has to give her own coin."

"But . . ." Amelia blinked, reaching into her reticule. "I'm not sure what I have."

"Coin," the ferryman repeated, holding out a clawlike hand.

"Certainly," Amelia said. "There is no need to be impatient." She delved deeper into her purse, muttering under her breath, "Or rude."

The ferryman laughed. "Styx and stones, missy. Styx and stones."

"Here, I have a coin," Amelia said in relief. She pulled out a ha'pence and held it out. "Will this be enough? It's all I have."

The ferryman took it and bit it. "All right. If you are sure you want ter cross."

"She does," Paris said quickly.

"Let the lady speak fer herself," the ferryman said.

"I-I do," Amelia said, a lump forming in her throat.

"Then come along," the ferryman said. Paris immediately jumped onto the boat. He held out his hand and Amelia took it.

"Amelia!" a voice shouted from behind.

Amelia paused, looking over her shoulder. She could not believe her eyes. Michael, dressed in his wedding suit, was waving madly and running toward her down the grassy slope.

Estelle, her white wedding dress hiked up to her knees, and her train trailing behind, chased behind him. "Michael!"

"Amelia!" Michael shouted again. "Stop. Do not go! I love you! I want to marry you!"

"What?" Amelia exclaimed, her heart pounding.

"Come with me, Amelia," Paris said. He jerked her forward. Amelia, surprised and offset, toppled into the boat with a screech. "Set sail, Charon!"

Amelia scrabbled up, lurching and swaying as she attempted to gain her footing. "No, Michael wants to marry me!"

"Sit down," Charon said. "Don't rock the boat!"

Amelia didn't pay him heed, but stumbled to the side, rocking the boat even farther. "Michael! Michael!"

"Oh, she's a live one," Charon said, driving his pole in and attempting to shove off from shore.

"Stop!" Amelia cried, careening into him and grabbing fast to the pole.

"Here now!" Charon exclaimed. "You'll toss us all in, and we'll be floating in the river between life and death."

"I don't care," Amelia cried, clinging to the pole all the tighter. "He wants to marry me!"

"Amelia!" Michael arrived at the bank, panting. "Don't go! You mustn't go!"

"Let me go to him!" Amelia cried, even as Paris reached for her.

"You've already paid the ferryman!" Charon cackled.

"No!" Michael cried. With a bounding leap, he cleared the distance and plummeted into the boat. Everyone cried out at the same time.

"Michael, you are mine," Estelle cried, arriving just behind him. She amazingly picked up her skirts and bolted onto the boat as well. The rickety craft rocked, swayed and dipped deep into the water. Utter chaos reigned a moment, as bodies untangled themselves from each other amidst shrieks and curses. Then everyone, with an innate instinct, froze, as the boat itself gave out a mighty, creaking groan.

"I love you, Amelia," Michael said, panting. "Marry me!"

"No, come with me, Amelia," Paris said, his tone urgent.

"Too many, too many," Charon said, angrily.

"Michael, you are mine," cried Estelle. "I won't release you!"

"Amelia," Paris said. "I am a prince. Come live with me in the Elysian Fields."

"What?" Estelle asked, her gaze turning to Paris. "You are a prince? And a landowner?"

"Marry me, Amelia," Michael said. "Live with me."

"I can shower you with riches," Paris said. "More than you can imagine. You will live like a queen."

"But what about Estelle?" Amelia asked.

"You are *that* rich?" Estelle breathed, gazing at Paris.

"Only two have fares," Charon snapped.

"I won't marry her," Michael said, shaking his head. "I love you. To hell with honor."

"I'm telling you, I ain't taking you there until you pay your fare," Charon said.

"I have power," Paris said urgently. "And it will be yours eternally."

"We haven't written our best work yet, Amelia," Michael said.

"Power? Eternally?" Estelle said. "You mean, like always?"

"We haven't, have we?" Amelia laughed.

"Time is running out," Charon shouted, his wizened face turning blue. He glared at them all. "And only two have fares."

"If you love me, Amelia," Michael said, "we must go now."

"I love you," Amelia said. "I have always loved you!"

"No, Amelia!" Paris cried. "You do not understand. I promised Hades he'd have you!"

"I'm not going with you," Amelia said to Paris. "I'm going to marry Michael."

"I'll go!" Estelle said quickly.

"I need a fare!" Charon said. "I'm telling you, I need a fare!"

"Here is my fare," Estelle said, jerking off her engagement ring and tossing it to Charon. Charon snatched it up in midflight.

"What?" Paris asked, staring at Estelle.

"Good-bye," Michael said, laughing. He moved swiftly, jumping from the boat safely onto the land. He turned, holding out his arms.

"Good-bye, Paris," Amelia giggled.

"Amelia, wait!" Paris cried out, his tone desperate.

Amelia only laughed all the more and jumped from the boat, stumbling into Michael's waiting arms.

"I have two! That's the ticket!" Charon shouted in triumph. He dug his pole in, and with what could only be a supernatural strength, shoved the boat far into the River Styx.

Amelia and Michael stood watching a moment. Estelle was already moving to sit close to Paris. Paris looked totally shocked. Charon was cackling, and striking up what sounded like an old sea shanty.

"Come, darling," Michael said. "And don't look back!"

They both turned and ran. Ran up the grassy slope. Ran through the odd, darkened landscape. Ran until they saw the light from the mouth of the cave. Then they were safely out, into the bright of day. Venus and Cupid stood, waiting for them.

Amelia blinked. "Venitia! What are you doing here? And your butler as well?"

"They are Venus and Cupid, dear," Michael said, grabbing up her hand.

"What?" Amelia asked, blinking.

"Yes," Venus said, lifting her chin. "I am the Goddess of Love."

"You . . ." Amelia looked at Michael in bewilderment. He nodded his head. "Oh, my!"

"Where is Estelle?" Cupid asked.

"She went with Paris," Amelia said, still stunned.

"She did?" Venus asked. She broke out laughing. She looked to Cupid. "My spell of love would not work upon her, but she went with Paris anyway, of her own free will. What a creature."

Michael grinned. "He was a prince. And rich. And powerful. He was a better man for her, I think."

"And she a better woman for him, if woman you can call her," Venus said, still chuckling. "Hades will think he has won a new soul. But she doesn't have one."

"Hades?" Amelia asked, her eyes widening.

"Yes, Hades," Michael said, his expression turning sober. "That was the River Styx Paris wanted to you cross, Amelia. He wanted to take you into the underworld."

Amelia choked. "The underworld?"

"It is both heaven and hell in mythology," Michael said softly. He glanced at Venus and Cupid. "Well, mythology is not the correct term, since it is clearly not a myth."

Amelia shook her head. "But I . . . I don't understand it all? How . . . why?"

"Let us just say," Cupid said quickly, "that Venus and I saw a reason to come to England for a visit. And things—"

"Did not go exactly as we planned," Venus finished.

"Paris—" Cupid began.

"Was not a good notion," Venus said, giving Cupid a

nod. She looked at Amelia. "Paris should never have done what he did. He said he did it out of love, but that he would take you to the underworld was not love. When Hades sided with him, it left us powerless."

Amelia stared at Venus. Then her gaze turned to Michael. Tears formed in her eyes. "So you came to get me?"

"Yes," Michael said. His face darkened. "I'm sorry, Amelia. I'm sorry that . . . that I almost married Estelle. I'm sorry that . . . that you thought you must run off with Paris. Can you ever forgive me?"

"Yes," Amelia said. She laughed slightly. "How can I not? You entered heaven and hell for me."

Michael's eyes flared and he laughed. "And you left heaven and hell for me."

"I love you," Amelia cried, and threw herself into Michael's arms. He caught her up and kissed her passionately. She returned that kiss with all her heart and soul.

"Er, I hate to interrupt," Amelia heard Cupid say. "But I fear I must."

Amelia, passion-dazed, drew back from Michael to look at Cupid. She flushed. "I'm sorry. Forgive us."

"No, no," Cupid said, his blue eyes twinkling. "It is very much what we like to see, but just not outside the cave to the underworld."

"Yes," Venus said. "Do let us leave before Hades discovers the exchange."

Michael pulled Amelia even closer. "How can I ever thank you? You saved Amelia for me."

Venus smiled. "You do not need to thank me. Consider it my gift to you."

Cupid laughed. "It is your Valentine's Day in England. It can be her valentine to you."

Venus laughed. "Yes. And if you truly wish to please me, then merely continue loving each other."

Amelia and Michael looked at each other. Amelia smiled, knowing she could safely make that promise, even to the Goddess of Love herself. "We will."

"Yes," Michael said, his gaze steady and sure upon her. "We will."

"Then farewell," Venus said. "Remember us always. We will remember you, won't we, Cupid?"

"Yes, Mother," Cupid said, offering a bow. "You did it, fair and square. You are indeed the best."

"I am, am I not?" Venus said, lifting her head proudly and laughing.

Amelia and Michael laughed as well, even as a bright shimmer of light engulfed them. Amelia closed her eyes from the sheer intensity of it. When she opened her eyes again, she was still in Michael's arms, but they were in his library. She looked around at the familiar room, the familiar desk. Then she looked at Michael.

His eyes were understanding. "Shocking, isn't it?"

"Yes," Amelia said, nodding. "Very."

Michael laughed, and shook his head, his gaze roving over to the desk. "You know, if we wrote this story, no one would ever believe us."

Amelia sighed and held him close. "You are right." Then she grinned. "But we can write about love for them, can't we?"

Michael nodded and, leaning down, kissed her. "Yes, we can. Every day of our lives, if you want."

"I do want," Amelia whispered, returning another, more fierce kiss. "Every day."

"Amelia," Michael said, pulling back and looking shocked.

Amelia laughed, happiness all but shimmering through every fiber of her body. "I may very well become a Lord Byron yet."

"No," Michael said, his eyes ardent. "You will become Lady Waverly, and that is that."

"Period," Amelia said, sighing in deep satisfaction. "That's it!"

Cupid's Ace

Jeanne Savery

The front door slammed. Charity Cliffe, by courtesy Lady Crandle and the future Lady Trenton, felt tension flow up her body at the angry steps stomping across the foyer.

Biting her lip, she lowered her head, concentrating on the tiny creation spread over her lap. With trembling fingers she set another stitch, but, seeing what she'd done and knowing she must remove it when her hands were better controlled, she set her needle.

Then, waiting, her fingers plucked at the soft material, twisted it . . .

On his last visit her father-in-law, Lord Trenton, had informed Charity that high wind and rain caused a leak in Trenton Hall's west wing's roof, resulting in much destruction. Then, with that chill, high-nosed manner that always made her feel she must be no better than a worm, he'd told her it was her duty to supply a new christening robe of such exquisite workmanship and excellent quality it would be used for generations to come. The manner of delivery was unpalatable to Charity.

So too was the underlying, unuttered, demand. *She was also, as quickly as humanly possible, to provide the babe which would be dressed in the new gown.* Still worse, was the implied question. Why, she heard, although it was never stated aloud, had she not yet begun to do so?

A sensible girl, Charity made no attempt to answer *that* impertinence!

Another door slammed. This time the sound came from upstairs and Charity relaxed. Her husband of just over four months had not come into the salon where she sat working. It would not be necessary, immediately, to endure a ranting scold on some imagined lack in her housekeeping or a rambling tirade on how it was *all her fault*.

Timon, Lord Crandle, was a trifle unclear on exactly how their marriage was her responsibility, but from the very beginning he'd insisted it was so. From the moment the two had been ordered into Lord Trenton's library where their fathers stood shoulder to shoulder and informed them their engagement would be announced and the wedding solemnized in less than a month, it was, according to Timon, all her fault!

Charity always recalled that particular afternoon with something akin to horror. No sooner had they been informed of their future happiness than they were dismissed. With a wolfish grin, a wink, and a slap to Timon's back which had him wincing, Charity's father told them to run along into the garden and plan their wedding journey.

Timon had grasped her wrist in a hold just a trifle too firm and practically pulled her over the low-silled window and into the sun-drenched garden. With her in tow, he'd marched, at far too rapid a pace for comfort, along the path and up the two steps into the folly his grandfather had built some fifty years previously.

"Why did you do it?"

"Why did I do what?" she'd asked.

"Talk those two into agreeing to this abomination!" He glared. The glare turned to suspicion. "Or *tricked* them, more like." He eyed her, seething. "Have you a bun in the oven, then?" he demanded after a moment.

"Have I *what?*"

"Got a bun in the oven."

"You know very well I never learned to cook!"

At her retort, he'd grinned a quick grin, but sobered instantly, and the glower returned. He waited, fists curled into his hips.

Charity put her nose in the air, and added, "I haven't a notion what you mean."

"Are . . . you . . . increasing," he said, enunciating each word clearly, his face practically thrust into hers.

Charity's chin came down. "Increasing! You mean *enciente?*" He nodded. Blushing rosily, she'd backed away. "You can't think . . ." she whispered. "You aren't suggesting . . ."

He followed, seeming to tower over her for all he'd only three inches on her. "You need a husband fast so you've convinced my tyrant of a father you'd make me a good wife?"

"Timon, I wouldn't do a thing like that. You know I wouldn't."

"Do I?" he said bitterly.

Timon had recently suffered a Disappointment in Love. Just when he'd come to the decision he could not live his life without her, the doxy he'd had in keeping told him to run along, that she'd found a *real* man, who would keep her in diamonds and carriages and give her a house with servants—just the way she'd always wanted.

"Women aren't to be trusted," he told Charity. *"You're a woman."*

"You are insulting."

"Am I? Well, we'll see. If you've a babe in arms any time in the next nine months, I'll repudiate it *and* you, do you hear me?"

"I wonder the whole world can't hear you!"

"Bah." He turned on his heel.

"Where are you going?"

"To London."

"London!"

"Where I'll drink a river of Blue Ruin and try to forget all this." Turning, backing away from her, he added, "I cannot believe my father would do this to me."

Charity saw the hurt, the alarm, the . . . the panic? . . . in her old friend's eyes. "I'll tell them I don't want to marry you," she offered quickly.

"After convincing them it is just the thing?"

She ran to catch him up. "But Timon, I was just as surprised as you when they made that announcement. I'd no hint anything of the sort was in the wind, or I would, somehow, have warned you. Truly."

He glared at her. "I don't believe you. They can't have come up with such a stupid plan all on their own."

"Timon Cliffe, you are impossible."

"Then I don't see why you want to marry me, and by all that's holy, you'll wish you hadn't."

He'd run from her, then, and disappeared. She hadn't seen him again until they met at the altar, where he'd growled out his responses with something akin to a snarl.

With a wry little smile Charity recalled how startled the

vicar had been! Still smiling sadly at the memory, she turned her eyes to the robe—and found the material crushed in her clenched fists. With a startled "Oh," she smoothed the wrinkles as best she could, checking that she hadn't damaged the tiny garment. She'd put far too much work into it, making row after row of tiny tucks running up and down the front and back of the bodice, each edged with the daintiest of lace. Then the lavish white-on-white embroidery around the long flowing skirts, which was so terribly difficult to do except in the *very* best light . . .

She gently touched the fine lawn and imagined it buttoned around the small form of her own babe. Would there, she wondered wistfully, ever be a babe . . . ? Her thoughts were interrupted by still another door slamming back against the wall. This time the salon door.

She sighed and raised her eyes. "Yes, Timon?"

He stalked over to the fireplace and laid an arm on it. "We are invited to the Montmorencys' Valentine Ball."

To her distress he still used the cold tones so unlike the warm affectionate voice she remembered. *This* voice, so like his father's, was all she'd heard since they were wed.

"I have decided to accept." He eyed his wife and grimaced. "You'll need a decent gown since those rags you wear appear to be all you've got in your wardrobe. I just looked." Before she could even think to accuse him of snooping, he added, "Go to Madam Vivian. Tomorrow. There is little enough time if she's to make you look as if you belonged at a *ton* ball!"

"But Timon . . ."

"No! Don't argue! Just do it."

"But Timon . . ."

"I won't have my wife looking such a dowd. I tell you I don't want to hear any . . ."

"Timon," she interrupted in a firm clear voice, "how am I to pay for it?"

Timon fell silent. "Pay for it."

"I can't purchase things if I cannot pay for them. That wouldn't be right."

"But your pin money . . ." he muttered. He stared, obviously thinking furiously. "Your dress allowance, your . . ." He glowered. "What have you done with it all?" His eyes widened, narrowed. "Have you already gambled your quarter's income away?" he demanded.

"What allowance? What pin money?" Her eyes widened. "I've an *income?*"

Timon stared at her and was rather unsettled by the huge eyes surrounded by long lashes somewhat darker than her hair. Hair which, as usual, was primly rolled up in a tight knot at the back of her head. He reminded himself she needed a new hairstyle as well as a gown!

"Your *allowance,* Cherry. *You* know."

Cherry! Her heart beat faster. It was the special name by which he'd always called her!

"But, Timon, I *don't* know."

"You mean m'father didn't explain it to you? You mean the reason you look like someone's great-aunt who hasn't gone into society for a century is that you really haven't a notion of the outrageous settlement made on you? Far beyond what you'll need for a new wardrobe each season?"

"A *settlement?*" Charity glowed. "You mean I've truly got my own *money?*"

"This isn't some stupid trick, is it?" His glower returned. "You *know* I didn't want to marry you." He flicked a disparaging look from her feet up to her head. "I thought you'd been dressing that way to get even. To get a little revenge?"

"Revenge?" Charity frowned. "Timon, what sort of trick?"

"You mean to tell me you *haven't* tried to make me feel

like a bug for leaving you alone so much?" He glowered really fiercely and pointed a finger at her. "Well, I think you *have*." But her frown punctured his certainty and the finger wavered in the face of an innocence which could not have been assumed.

"Timon," she said, "I truly didn't know I could pay for a new wardrobe. No one ever explained any of that to me. I've only *pretended* I'd housekeeping money and that I knew what I was about and your housekeeper seemed to think I did and, so far, that's all worked out all right."

"She isn't *my* housekeeper," snapped Timon, back on his high horse. "M'father found her and the other servants *and* the house." He recalled *why* he was forced to reside in a *house*. "You don't think I lived like this before our marriage, do you?" he ranted, and went on with one of his more common complaints. "No, I did not. I'd a set of snug rooms like all the other fellows. I came and went as I pleased, and no one cared. I didn't worry about mud on my boots or if I spilled something or whether I'd trip over some maid cleaning the stairs! And furthermore . . ."

"Did you?" asked Charity, interrupting. She'd heard all but that last bit before.

"Blast it, woman, now I've lost my place."

"But Timon, *did* you?"

"Did I what?

"Trip over a maid?" Her huge eyes sparkled, and she raised her hands to hide a smile.

"Don't you dare laugh. It isn't the least bit funny. I might have fallen and broken my neck and been *killed*."

"Nonsense, Timon. You are much too agile. But the poor maid. Did you bruise her badly with your great huge boots?"

"Lord, I hadn't thought of that." He tried to remember just how and *where* he'd come into contact with the apologetic little maid who had, after all, only been doing her work when he raced up the stairwell, rounded the corner at the first landing, and practically fallen all over her. He'd been rather nasty, he remembered, berating her for being in his way . . .

Oh blast, something else about which he must feel guilty!

"Timon," asked Charity shyly, those big eyes holding his, "will *you* take me to Madam Vivian's?"

His rampaging thoughts once again interrupted, he stared down his nose at her.

Quickly, Charity added, "Please?"

It occurred to Timon that, if he wished his wife to shine at the ball, he'd better take a hand in designing her gown. Left to herself she'd probably order a plain white muslin tied with a pink ribbon or something equally frugal, to say nothing of exceedingly inappropriate to her married state. He scowled.

"Be ready at eleven," he ordered. "I won't wait for you."

"I'll be ready. Oh, Timon, thank you. You've no notion how I've wanted new gowns." She plucked at the sensible cotton, not at all sheer or particularly well dyed, making up the one she wore. "I hate the things Biddy chose, but, Timon, she *wouldn't listen*. I *told* her they were all wrong."

It hadn't occurred to Timon to wonder where or when or how Charity had been prepared for her marriage. And it *should* have crossed his mind. After all, one of the things which had drawn them together when they were children was the fact each had lost a mother at an early age.

"Your father's doddering old housekeeper had a hand in choosing your brideclothes?" he asked, astounded.

"Yes. I wanted to come to London to my aunt, but my father said she wasn't here and, besides, the notion was all a lot of nonsense and far too expensive and that I'd very likely need very little since we'd be living . . ." Her eyes widening to their widest, Charity covered her mouth tightly, clasping both hands over it.

Timon's glare returned, his mouth settling into a grim line. Very obviously Charity had nearly let another cat out of the bag. He wasn't about to let it get shoved out of sight and tied back up until he'd discovered what else his father had planned in order to ruin his life—besides, of course, the married state he'd not yet been ready to adopt.

"We'd be living . . . ?" he asked in that chilling voice which she hated. "You know you might as well tell me. I'll get it out of you in the end . . . !"

"Your father told me we'd be living in the country," she divulged. "At Mumford Manor." She hung her head as if it were her fault their parents had planned that bit as well as their wedding.

"Mumford Manor. *Completely* isolated from anywhere interesting? Right out *in the middle of the country?* Only *ten miles* from *Trenton Hall?*" With each question his voice rose until, with the final question, he nearly roared: *"Nowhere near London?"*

"Timon, it wasn't my idea. I was *glad* when you said we'd live here. Truly."

Timon eyed her thoughtfully. "I remember m'father balked when I told him . . ."

". . . Told him?"

Timon grimaced. "He came up to town to drag me home for those weeks before our marriage. I refused to go, of course, and informed him then there would be no bride-journey, that I would bring you straight up to London." His lips compressed, and he stared over her head. "I seem to recall he tried to talk me out of it . . ."

"Well, you talked him *into it,* so that's all right."

"You really don't mind? Not having a bridal trip?"

"Timon, I've *enjoyed* London, going places, seeing things. I've been to the Tower and the menagerie and saw the paintings at the Exhibition and I even managed to see the last balloon ascension! Oh, Timon, it was wonderful and I almost missed it because I didn't know about it until the very last minute, you see, and . . .'' Charity's excitement faded at the look on her husband's face.

"This isn't the country. You can't just traipse around, going wherever the fancy takes you! Charity Morris, you'd better be able to tell me you didn't go alone to all those places! Or . . .'' A thought struck him and he asked, hopefully, ''. . . perhaps your aunt took you?''

''Charity *Cliffe,* if you please, and even if it *doesn't.* Please you, that is, which I know it doesn't, and,'' she continued in a bit of a rush when he looked still angrier, ''my aunt is in Naples, as you very well know, so she couldn't, even if she wished. Take me, I mean.'' Very much on her dignity, Charity continued, ''Besides, you shouldn't assume I know *absolutely nothing* about how to go on. I always take George, my footman. And Black is a *very* good coachman, an excellent driver, never drunk you know, and not at all belligerent or anything like that, the way so many coachies are. He's chapel bred, which is a very good thing in a coachman, I think. Besides, he knows where a lady *shouldn't* go and *twice* he's told me I mustn't do something I very much wished to do.''

''Oh?'' Timon made a mental note to thank his coachman for having a care to his wife's reputation.

''I wished to see the dandies sitting in the bow window at White's—''

Timon groaned softly at the thought of what would have been said if his wife had been seen driving down St. James's anytime later than ten in the morning!

''—And a few weeks ago I heard there was to be a race . . .''

Charity turned her eyes sideways, toward her husband, and then quickly away. She'd learned, by overhearing his valet speaking with her maid, that Timon was to race his famous sorrels against one of his friends who had purchased a new team. She'd very much wished to be there to cheer him on. But Black told her, in that kindly, almost fatherly way of his, that her presence would not be appreciated by the bucks.

So, instead, she'd gone to Hatchard's and spent a few of her carefully hoarded coins to buy a second book by the lady who wrote *Sense and Sensibility*. She'd been tempted by one of Byron's newest works, something called *The Giaour*, as well, but sensibly, if ruefully, had decided she mustn't waste her money since she'd so little of it.

Except Timon had just told her she had *lots* of spending money. "Timon," she said, an urgency in her tone, "when we are finished at Madam Vivian's, can we go to Hatchard's? There are *several* books I've wished to purchase but have not dared do so because I feared to spend the little money I had. So, can we? Please?"

Timon's guilt rose up to choke him. "Blast and bedamned to you Charity Morris! Do you have to make me feel like a worm at every turn?" He stalked across the salon.

"Charity Cliffe," she whispered to his back.

Charity, wincing beforehand in expectation, waited for the door to slam. She was greatly surprised when it did not, but was closed with great care, almost silently, in fact.

Then, moments later, the front door banged.

Which made her jump.

"Oh, Timon, do you really think I dare wear such a gown?"

They'd just left Madam Vivian's, and Charity took several skipping steps to catch up with her husband, who had so nonchalantly and competently ordered her ball gown from the frighteningly severe Madam Vivian.

Madam Vivian had taken one arrogant, disbelieving, to

say nothing of dismissive, look at Charity's awful gown and turned to Timon, whom she seemed to know—which rather surprised Charity. But then Timon, in a rather embarrassed fashion, had introduced her as Lady Crandle, and Madam, her eyes narrowed, had studied the bride.

It had seemed to Charity the modiste looked right through her dress. Which was terribly embarrassing. She hadn't liked the expression on the modiste's face and had raised her chin. She'd then seen a very odd gleam appear in the modiste's eye. The woman had turned to Timon and launched into a harangue on *what would suit,* to which he'd listened respectfully, objecting only once or twice, and offering only one or two suggestions of his own.

And then, when they'd agreed on a design for the ball gown, Madam had suggested that perhaps his wife required one or two other gowns. But, by then, Timon was bored. After agreeing that his wife was quite obviously in need of a great many more than one or two, he suggested Charity make an appointment and return another day. Then Madam could tell her what was proper.

Madam grimaced, rolled her eyes, and mouthed, "Men!"

Charity, recalling that scene, giggled and decided that perhaps Madam wasn't quite so formidable after all. So now she and Timon were walking down Piccadilly to Number 190. Together.

At breakfast that morning, Timon had informed her she could have a whole half hour to browse amongst the books while he laid his glims on the news sheets laid out for that purpose on a table near the fireplace.

"I mean," he'd said when she'd looked confused, "while I run my eye over the newspapers."

But Hatchard's! Charity could barely believe Timon had actually told her she might purchase whatever she wanted. *As many books as she wanted!* It was unbelievable. She'd almost smiled when he'd spoken in that airy fashion she remembered from when they were children and he'd done something to hurt her and then wanted to apologize without actually saying the words . . .

Was he, she wondered wistfully, beginning to like her again?

After breakfast, while her maid did her hair, Charity wrote out a list of the books she knew she wanted. She'd give the list to one of Hatchard's exceedingly helpful clerks and ask that he collect them while she used her precious half hour to search out books she didn't, as yet, know existed.

Oh, it was all quite wonderful! Charity gave a little hop and then, when Timon glared at her, she hunched her shoulders very slightly and smiled a tiny tight little smile. In other words, she managed to control her elation, except for the sparkle in her eyes, to the point she could stroll along beside him in a properly demure fashion.

Even Timon's very best glare couldn't dampen her feelings today!

Timon yawned.

"Tired so early?" asked his friend Robin, shuffling the cards.

Timon picked up a stack of coins and let them slip, clinking, through his fingers and back to the baize-topped table. "Up early," he admitted. "Told Cherry to go to Madam Vivian, but she was afraid, so had to take her myself."

"To . . . Madam Vivian?" Robin's eyes rather boggled.

"What's wrong with Madam? She dresses the very highest in the *ton!*"

"She also," said Robin, his voice dry as dust, "dresses the lowest. Your mistress, for instance."

"*Dressed* my mistress. When I *had* a mistress. Past tense, Rob!" The frown, which was beginning to leave a permanent line between his eyes, returned to mar Timon's classic features. "Before the whore told me . . ."

His mouth snapped shut. Even to his closest friend Timon couldn't admit exactly what the doxy had said. A *real* man indeed! What made a man a real man, anyway? he wondered. Then he yawned again.

"So—" Robin, who had met the bride long before she'd become a bride, when visiting Timon's home as a youth, pictured the waiflike female creature with a rather startling strength of mind. For a girl. "—you took Lady Crandle to Madam Vivian. She didn't object?"

"Why should she object?"

So much for her strength of mind. The creature he recalled wouldn't have put up with being *told*. So, instead, Robin reminded his friend of one of his complaints. "You informed me," said Robin, with the air of explaining something to the village idiot, "that your wife was dressing herself as badly as possible just to spite you."

"Oh. Well . . . as to that"— Timon felt his ears heating up—"I *think* I may have been *wrong.*"

"No. Never. Not *you.*"

Timon ignored Robin's mild sarcasm and described the scene between himself and his wife. ". . . So you see, I think perhaps she just didn't know what to do."

"Maybe you need to teach her."

"*Me?*" Timon blinked. "*Me!* I don't know how a bride should go on! What she *needs* is an older *ton*nish woman to set her right."

"Find one."

"Now?"

"Why not?"

"Robin, it's been four months!" The heat which had faded from Timon's ears returned to his whole face. "If

I'd done it right away, well, then it would've made sense, but *now*?"

"See what you mean," said Robin thoughtfully. "Embarrassing at this point. Well, then, you'll have to do it."

"Are you suggesting . . ."

"Shush! Lower your voice!"

Timon looked around Boodle's game room and saw that he'd drawn attention, disturbing serious gamblers and rousing the curiosity of those prone to gossip.

"Let's go," he snarled. He rose to his feet, pocketing the coins lying around the table.

"Go where?"

"I don't know. Your place?"

Robin hesitated, then shrugged. "All right."

Once out on the pavement and headed for Robin's rooms in the Albany, Timon returned to exactly where they'd left off. "You can't be suggesting I should take her around to boring at-homes and squire her to slow-top entertainments where they expect one to pay attention to squealing squeaking girls attempting to sing and out-of-tune pianofortes and places where men spout poetry and all that sort of thing? You can't mean that."

"Why not? Get her vouchers for Almack's as well."

"Oh yes, just the thing! And then," said Timon scornfully, "you think I should escort her there. Would *you* go to Almack's if you weren't occasionally dragged there by your mother?"

"Actually, yes." Timon boggled at that, and Robin sighed. "We're a bit different in that, you know. I *like* to dance. And I don't mind the chicken stakes one plays for there. I only gamble because it's the thing to do."

"You think I gamble for any other reason?"

"You aren't one of the guns who will bet huge amounts on just about anything, but you *do* like to have a flutter going here and there most all the time. And you very often think the evening ill spent if you've not sat in at one of the tables where the wagers are well beyond *my* pocket."

"So now, on top of all else, I'm a wastrel running through my inheritance, am I?" stormed Timon.

"I didn't say that. In fact I'm pretty certain you never lose much more than you can afford, but Timon—" Robin turned his eyes sideways, wondering if he dared say what he'd been wanting to say for some time now—"you are losing more than you used to do and maybe . . ."

"Maybe one day I'll lose everything and end up in the fleet? I doubt it. I don't enjoy it *that* much." Timon plodded along, his shoulders hunched. "Do you suppose that's why m'father decided to marry me off? He hoped to set my head in a different direction?"

"Could be. Fathers get odd notions, as I know to my sorrow!"

Timon ignored the hint his friend had had a run in with his own father. "Which reminds me! Another thing I just learned is that m'father had it planned that we'd live in the country. Can you believe that? About as far from London as one can get?"

"Trenton Hall isn't *that* far away. And maybe he thinks it time you began taking on some of the work. You aren't alone in that. *M'father* has warned me that I'm to come home at the end of this season and take over the management of the farms. He means to oversee the construction of the new bridge and oversee the work on the canal in which he's invested. He says there will be quite enough to keep the both of us busy . . ."

"*My* father isn't building any canals or bridges. Don't see why he needs me. Besides, he doesn't want me doing things. Remember how he wouldn't turn the stables over to me when I wanted . . ."

"Yes," interrupted Robin, "but *that* was because you

wanted to raise and train racehorses. Make a splash in racing circles!"

Timon felt his skin heating up again. He now knew far more about the rather elastic moral tone in the racing world. It *had* been a rather foolish notion. "Oh well . . ."

"Here we are." Robin threw open the door to his two rooms and, as Timon passed through, bowed in a mocking manner. "Welcome to my humble abode."

Timon stopped short. Had his own rooms been so cluttered, this . . . messy? He watched Robin move with practiced ease around a small table, sidle between two overstuffed chairs, and step over a pile of riding boots, short boots, and shoes, all of which were badly in need of polishing.

Robin reached the sideboard and searched among the ale pots, dirty glasses, and mugs. "Malley!" he yelled.

There was no response from Robin's man. Which wasn't unusual. Timon wondered why his friend hadn't, long ago, fired the valet-cum–everything else. *He'd* have done so . . .

. . . or would he? With great effort Timon recalled the frustrations of tight quarters, his clothes never where they should be, the coat which he'd want instantly still unbrushed and unironed, dirty dishes littering the tables, and his man almost never where he was supposed to be.

"Sorry, Timon. I don't know where Malley's gotten to. Doesn't seem to be a clean glass or mug . . . I'll rinse one out."

Somehow the thought of grubby glassware didn't appeal. "Never mind, Rob. I'm not thirsty."

"Or we could drink out of the bottle," suggested Robin, and tossed one toward his friend. "In case you've gotten so high in the instep that you've forgotten, living as you do now, it's what we'd do at your place in the old days."

Timon barely reacted in time to avert disaster. He just managed to catch the bottle and sighed, half in relief he'd caught it and half for the frustration that it was necessary. But it *was* what they'd always done when there were no clean cups or mugs or what-have-you. And he'd thought it the best of good fun.

So when had he changed? Thoughtfully, he pulled the cork and took a swig, swallowed . . . coughed and choked . . . and finally managed to control himself. His eyes watered, and he peered at what he held.

"What is this?"

"Oops! Wrong tipple," said Robin with a weak grin. "Meant to toss you the wine, not the gin . . ."

Timon stared at the bottle. "When did you start drinking Blue Ruin?"

"Oh, I don't know . . ." Robin wouldn't meet his eyes.

"Since you heard you had to go home come summer?" guessed Timon.

Robin drew in a deep breath and let it out a bit shakily. "We're a pair, aren't we, Timon? We've had a good run of fun since coming down from Oxford and now we're objecting when we're told it is time to grow up and act responsibly. Bound to happen, of course. Just didn't think it would be quite so soon . . . ?"

"Spoiled brats, you'd say?" asked Timon, thoughtfully. "Hmm."

Timon sighed in turn, and looked around. One of the chairs had nothing more than a jacket thrown over the back. He added it to the pile filling the other. Sitting, he laid his head back and stared at the ceiling. The *dirty* ceiling . . . He put that thought from his mind.

"Robin," he said, "I am so very tired of feeling guilty."

"Why do you feel guilty?"

Timon hesitated before making the admission. "I haven't treated Cherry well. I was furious at m'father and have been taking my anger out on her."

"Haven't beat her or anything like that, have you?"

"Worse, maybe. I've ignored her. She looks at me with those great big eyes and . . . and I run."

"Why?"

"Don't know. Funny, really. Always thought that when I got around to it, I'd marry my Cherry. And now I have. And I act as if it were her fault."

"That's what you said when you came tearing up to town. Said she'd talked the old men into arranging it all."

"I don't suppose I really believed it even then."

"So?"

"So"—Timon hunched down deeper into the chair—"I don't know . . ."

Something poked him, and he lifted himself enough to feel under his back, where he found a small statue of a horse. He stared at it. Nothing ever poked him when he sat down in his bedroom at home! He stared, again, at the soot-darkened ceiling and was forced to admit there *were* advantages to having a house overseen by a woman who knew how things should be done, making things comfortable and . . .

No! He *would not* think anything good had come from his marriage . . .

. . . Or would he?

Settling back, his elbows on the chair arms, Timon held the horse in both hands and toyed with it. "I just don't know what to do for the best," he muttered. "I just don't know . . ."

"I told you . . ."

"Almack's! You can come up with a better notion than that!"

"But you don't like my *better* idea either," muttered Robin, eyeing his friend.

* * *

"It's quite all right, Lady Crandle," said Robin, sooth-ingly. "I've been to see my aunt, and she says she would very much like to meet you."

Charity looked up, wide-eyed, at her husband's tall friend. "It's just that I'm not certain what Timon will think . . . ?"

Robin didn't care what Tim thought. What he himself thought was that Tim was a fool. His little wife was a delightful little lady, very easy on the eyes and, obviously, very much in love with her husband. Robin felt just the faintest twinge of envy and buried it under a silent tirade against Timon for being such an idiot.

"Mr. Mastwell, you know Timon," said Charity, inter-rupting him in the middle of his most poetic, if silent, denunciation. "Very likely," she admitted, albeit reluc-tantly, "you know him better than I do these days. Please assure me you truly feel I'm doing the right thing. Visiting your aunt, I mean."

"Need to know the ladies, Lady Crandle. M'aunt will do the proper and introduce you around. Not a question of how Timon feels about it."

Charity sighed and stopped, standing stock-still. A few paces later Robin realized she wasn't beside him and turned, strolled back, a query in his look. "I think I'd better go home," she said, her eyes sad-looking.

"I don't."

"But you don't understand. Timon . . ."

"Tim won't eat you whatever you do. He isn't that sort."

"I don't like it when he frowns so," said Charity softly. "He's so unhappy, Mr. Mastwell, and I can't like that at all. He says it's all my fault. I simply *mustn't* do anything which will make him more angry with me, don't you see?"

"Whatever Tim *says*, he doesn't *really* blame you for your marriage," said Robin quickly. "Believe me. I *do* know *that*. I don't pretend to understand what's going on in his head, but he admitted that much."

Charity felt a blush rushing into her cheeks. Timon had been talking about her, about their marriage . . . well, what could she expect. Robin, as she very well knew, had been Timon's best friend from their school days at Eton. She sighed. "I just don't know what to do for the best . . ."

"Which," said Robin, "is exactly what Tim said a day or so ago. But *I* know. You must meet the biddies, Lady Crandle, and find friends, that's what you must do."

"And your aunt is . . . is kind and . . . not . . . not . . ."

"Twitty? Not at all. She's the very best of aunts."

Charity drew in a deep breath. "I'll do it. I'll go with you and meet her."

"Excellent." Robin beamed at her and offered his arm.

They walked on, talking and laughing and very rapidly becoming the best of friends.

Timon, on his way to join the other members of the Four-in-Hand club for a Thursday drive down to Salt Hill, saw them but didn't recognize the fashionable young lady on Robin's arm. He knew the tall footman following the pair, however! Taking a second look, he was both astonished by his wife's extremely well-formed figure shown to perfection by her new gown, and by her enticing face and, simultaneously, he was absolutely furious she was looking up at Robin with that happy expression.

Why did she no longer look at him that way?

Timon was well beyond them before he admitted he'd given his wife no reason to look at him with that glowing look. Except . . . she had when they'd gone to Madam Vivian's and on to Hatchard's, had she not? But then, he recalled, he's wiped the smile from her face the instant they'd arrived home, by telling her, in the most sarcastic of tones, to be careful or she'd get a reputation as a blue-stocking.

Timon turned down a side street, turned again, and very soon had returned his team of matched bays demanded by the rules of FHC to their stables. Quite suddenly he'd no interest in joining the line of yellow-bodied barouches which would make their way at a strict trot to Salt Hill where the top sawyers would dine and then return in exactly the same way. Boring. Very boring . . . Even Timon recognized the irony in that: It had once been the height of his ambition to be elected to membership in the FHC!

He unsettled the whole household by stomping in at an hour when he was never home and plopping into a chair in the salon, a room he entered as rarely as he possibly could. Only much later did it occur to him that, although angry that Robin was squiring Charity somewhere, heaven only knew where, it had not once crossed his mind to suspect either of them of dalliance. Which, given how wonderful Charity looked in her new walking gown, it should have!

When it did occur to him, it also occurred to him that there was something quite important in that fact. Unfortunately, he was still too angry to come to grips with exactly what it was.

When Lady Heatherton's butler announced Lady Crandle and her own nephew, the lady laid aside her embroidery and rose to her feet, a smile on her face. Her eyes widened, and she came forward, her hands extended. *"My dear child,* you are the *image* of your mother!"

"My . . . mother?"

"Oh, the very dearest friend. I would have called on you long ago, my dear, but propriety said no. It was too soon after your wedding. Young people need those first months alone . . ." She sobered at the suddenly sad look on Charity's face. "My dear . . . ?"

There was so much sympathy in her ladyship's tone that, quite suddenly and definitely without her permission or expectation, Charity felt a hot tear run down her cheek, another, and then a stream. At the edge of her pain, she heard Lady Heatherton send her nephew off to the library and then, quite without knowing how it happened, she found herself in her ladyship's arms, her face pressed into the taller woman's lilac-scented shoulder and all sorts of encouraging noises telling her it was quite all right to cry and that she should get it all out of her system and that they would see what could be done to mend things and . . . and many other like words of understanding.

"Now," said Lady Heatherton when, much restored by her weeping, Charity was seated beside her with a cup of hot, well-sugared, tea, "you will tell me all and we will see what can be done about it."

Charity averted her eyes. "There is nothing to tell and nothing to be done either." She took a quick look at her disbelieving hostess. *"Really."*

Lady Heatherton chuckled. "Now there's a bouncer if I ever heard one! You don't fib very well, my dear, and it might be better if you did not try. However that may be, since you do not wish to say it, I will make a guess. Dear Timon did not like his father arranging his marriage and, since he is frightened of Trenton, he has taken it out on *you.*"

Charity's eyes widened. "You are a sorceress!"

"Not at all. I just happen to know Trenton very well. And, because his son is a friend of my nephew, I also know your Timon. Trenton, bless him, always had the tact of a toad." Her ladyship got a thoughtful look. "Actually, I believe he has *less.* Tact, I mean."

Charity giggled. "I don't blame Timon for being fright-

ened of him. His lordship scares me to death, *too*. And
Timon *hasn't* taken it out on me, my lady. He hasn't,'' said
Charity sadly, ''done anything at all with me.'' Once again
she got that faintly guilty look and glanced, quickly, at her
hostess. ''At least not much. Not until recently, I mean.
He took me to Madam Vivian's and then to Hatchard's,
where he said he'd give me a whole half hour, only he got
interested in a discussion between a couple of parliamen-
tarians and''—her eyes glowed in that way they had—''we
stayed *more than an hour,* which was wonderful.''

''You are a . . . scholar?'' asked Lady Heatherton, the
faintest of distasteful looks on her face.

''Oh no. I like to read, but''—Charity got rather red in
the face—''only *frivolous* things, you know. I bought Lord
Byron's *The Giaour,* for instance. It is,'' she added, quickly,
''very strange, is it now?''

Lady Heatherton ignored what was obviously a red her-
ring. ''Only frivolous things?'' she demanded.

Charity sighed. ''My father would have liked it if he
could have made a scholar of me, but I fear I'll never live
up to his expectations. I think, when it occurred to him
that perhaps Trenton might accept me as a wife for Timon,
he felt a great deal of relief. I've been a major disappointment to him I think.''

''Because you've the good sense not to become a blue-
stocking!''

Charity giggled, her hands over her mouth. ''He
wouldn't think of it in quite that way, my lady.''

''I am sure he would not. But this is far and fair off the
topic. What,'' she said, studying her guest, ''are we to do
about the situation as it stands? I don't quite feel I can sit
Timon down and give him a lecture on the proper treatment of his bride,'' she mused, ''so we won't do that. Now
I wonder . . . have you vouchers to Almack's?''

Charity shook her head, her eyes widening.

"Not? Ah! That I can put right. I will bring one or two of the patronesses along one afternoon to meet you. Lady Jersey will come. She has the greatest curiosity, you know, and will not be able to resist being among the first to meet Timon's bride. You must be very demure and wide-eyed and, if she asks impertinent questions, pretend you do not understand her. Perhaps I'll ask Lady Cowper as well. She is the kindest lady. You will like her. And, what is better, I believe she too knew your mother rather well."

"My mother's friends . . . I don't suppose," mused Charity, "that I ever wondered about her life before she married. It is a terrible thing to say, but it is difficult to even remember what she looked like." She glanced at Lady Heatherton to see if the lady was shocked by the admission but saw only kindly understanding. Shyly, she added, "I wish someday, when you've nothing better to do, you would tell me what you remember of her. Perhaps she will become more real to me if I know more about her?"

"A very good notion. We will have that talk, but not until we've got you properly settled into society. It is really too bad that your aunt took herself off to Naples just when she was needed."

"But she didn't know she'd be needed, did she?" excused Charity quickly. She felt a trifle guilty because she had, more than once, wished her father's sister had not departed for foreign climes just when she did.

"I think," said Lady Heatherton once she'd expressed agreement, "that when you've been approved by the patronesses I will hold a sort of soiree to which I will invite only ladies. In that way you may meet other young wives and some of their mothers and begin to make friends . . ."

"Timon has accepted an invitation to the Montmorencys' ball," said Charity. "Is it possible . . . do you think perhaps . . . ? She realized she could not possibly ask such a favor and her voice trailed off.

But her hostess wasn't at all put out. "Do I think," she said, for her guest, "that we can do all that before the ball so that you will not feel so alone when you attend it? Hmm ..." Lady Heatherton pursed her lips, her eyes focusing on nothing at all. She counted, silently, on her fingers and then nodded. Once. Firmly. "I believe it can be managed," she said. "My soiree will not be quite so large as I'd thought, but perhaps that is preferable. If too many came, not only would there be no cachet for those who meet you, but you would have no opportunity to get to know any of the guests! Hmmm, can you be at home tomorrow and the next day?"

Charity didn't hesitate. Actually, she didn't *have* to hesitate. "I've fittings in the early mornings for the ball gown, but I can easily be at home in the afternoons."

"Then expect Lady Jersey and perhaps Lady Cowper, and myself of course, to drop by tomorrow or the next day." Lady Heatherton frowned. "I've the impression Lady Jersey has a partiality for macaroons." She cast Charity a mischievous smile. "Perhaps you could ask your cook to be certain there are some?"

"I am certain quite excellent macaroons are not beyond her capability," said Charity with a completely sober face—but her eyes twinkled. When Lady Heatherton laughed delightedly, Charity chuckled. "Oh, I do like you," she exclaimed.

"And I like you, too." Her ladyship poured herself another cup of tea after ascertaining that Charity had had her fill. "Now, I believe we've settled a great deal. Shall I call in my nephew and tell him what he is to do?"

"What *he* is to do? But ..."

"If your husband is too ... hmm ... occupied to take you driving in the park, for instance, then Robin must do it. After you've met the patronesses, of course. He can then introduce you to some of the bucks, who will be sure to ask you for a dance at the ball. And he will," she added, very seriously indeed, "point out to you the men you must avoid. There aren't many men who would ruin a lady as fast as they'd look at look at one, but such villains do exist. It is a game with them, you see. But we will put you on your guard . . . Ah, Robin," she purred, as her nephew walked back into the room. "We were just talking about you . . ."

Lady Jersey ate several of the macaroons and compli-mented Charity on their texture. When she and Lady Cow-per had asked a handful of questions and drunk their tea and Lady Jersey, speaking softly but quickly and with a delightful insouciance, had passed on several of the latest *on dits,* the two patronesses looked at each other.

"I think . . . ?" asked Lady Jersey.

"Oh yes. I knew her mother, of course. A lovely friend before she married and hid herself in the country. You, my dear," said Lady Cowper, smiling at Charity, "remind me of her. The same sweet eyes with that hint of wistfulness, but also just a hint of impishness as well . . . Oh yes, vouch-ers, of course, and, my dear, I'll be sure to send you an invitation to my Venetian breakfast which is a day or two after the Montmorencys' Valentine Ball."

Lady Jersey, not to be outdone—in fact, in order to get in first—said that invitations to her musical, to be held a few days hence, would be delivered that afternoon by hand, and then her ladyship rose to her feet.

The three ladies left, but Lady Heatherton soon returned.

"Well!" she said. "That turned out very well, I think. I have returned to tell you that I forgot to say I'll pick you up in my carriage and take you to Lady Jersey's entertain-ment." She reached for a macaroon.

Charity, realizing it was Lady Heatherton's fourth or perhaps her fifth, made a mental note that Robin's aunt was very partial to the sweet. Lady Jersey might or might not have a special liking for them, but she would certainly remember to serve them whenever Lady Heatherton came to visit!

"Their ladyships are so very nice," said Charity. "I was frightened to death at the thought of entertaining such great ladies, but it wasn't so very difficult . . . And I haven't thanked you for arranging it!"

"They were nice to you because it would be difficult *not* to be nice to you. Lady Jersey, in particular, can be . . . difficult."

Charity smiled as she recalled The Jersey's slightly malicious stories. "She . . . gossips?"

Lady Heatherton laughed. "My dear, she isn't known as *Silence* for no reason!" Then her ladyship sobered. "You did well, my dear. I had primed them so that they'd not expect you to have gone about much, newly married and all . . . although I had a bit of difficulty explaining why your silly chub of a husband is still seen in his clubs and doing the things young unmarried men do."

"How did you explain it?" asked Charity, unable to think of a single excuse.

"Why, that he was giving you time to adjust to your new status, and thinking you very young, hadn't pressed you to take your place in society. But now that you've expressed an interest he's decided to begin taking you about and that the Montmorencys' ball would be your introduction to the *ton*."

"And you managed to say all that with a perfectly straight face?" asked Charity, a wondering look on her face . . . which soon collapsed into giggles. "I think I owe you more than mere thanks," she said when she could speak again.

The door to the salon was opened just then and her

butler, after clearing his throat, announced Mr. Mastwell. Robin strolled in, looking from his aunt to Charity and back again. "I see their great ladyships didn't eat either of you," he teased.

"Have you come to escort your aunt home?" asked Charity.

"Er . . ." He turned to Lady Heatherton. "Aunt?"

"I haven't had time to tell her, Robin."

"Tell me what?"

"Why that Robin will now take you for that drive in the park I mentioned to you! You've met two very important ladies, and all went very well. The next step is for you to meet a few gentlemen who will ask you for a dance at the ball. We mustn't allow you to be a wallflower, my dear. I'll introduce you to more partners when we go to the musicale, but very likely they won't be of quite the right stamp to add to your consequence, which the men Robin introduces you to will do. So, my dear, run up and change into a driving dress and put on your most charming bonnet. Robin will wait here."

Charity fervently, if silently, thanked heaven that she'd a brand-new and very charming bonnet to wear as well as a lovely new driving dress!

Timon, exercising another of his raking sorrels—a hunter he hoped to have ready for the fall cubbing—noticed Robin driving a neat open carriage which he finally recognized as Robin's aunt's town drag. The carriage was surrounded by a number of men, more than one of whom was laughing at something said by the lady at Robin's side.

Timon frowned. He's assumed it would be Robin's aunt, but this spritely little lady was certainly *not* the tall, well-padded Lady Heatherton! Timon approached and had very nearly reached the group when he heard a feminine giggle. A giggle he knew very well and, without thinking why, he turned his mount and returned the gelding to his stables.

When the front door opened and Charity tripped in he was pacing the salon. Actually, he'd been pacing for some time, his anger growing. He heard the butler's muttered request that Charity attend the master in the salon and heard her sigh. He also heard how her quick steps turned to a rather dragging pace and became still more angry that the need to face him took away all the happiness she'd gotten from her ride. She'd barely closed the door when he spoke.

"So! Flirting with every rake in London, I suppose," he said, nastily.

"I don't think so," she responded. "I mean, I don't suppose they were all rakes or that they included every rake in London."

"Don't widen those great eyes at me! I know when I'm being bamboozled, Charity Morris."

"Charity Cliffe, Timon. Please remember I'm no longer Charity Morris!"

"How can I forget?" He waved a hand to take in the ambience around them. "I live here, do I not?"

"But if you *don't* forget, why do you call me by my maiden name?"

"Because I . . . No! No red herrings, Charity. *You* will explain *to me* how Robin had the nerve to take you driving in the park without my permission?"

"How can I?"

"How can you what?"

"Explain how he had the nerve. I don't know, do I?"

"Blast and be damn . . ." Timon shut his mouth with a snap. "Don't take me so literally."

"But Timon, since you know I always do so, that is more nonsense. So what is it you really want to know?"

"Why he didn't tell me he meant to take you driving!"

"Again I can't tell you. I do know that his aunt ordered him to introduce me to his friends so I'd have dancing partners when . . ."

"And how—" Timon glared as he interrupted her—"do you know his aunt?"

"She knew my mother. Oh, Timon, it is so wonderful. She says she'll tell me what my mother was like when she was my age and . . ."

"Lady Heatherton came here to meet you?"

Charity's excitement faded. "No."

"Then . . . ?"

Charity told him what had occurred. ". . . said I'm to have vouchers and they will send invitations. Lady Jersey is giving a musical evening only two day's hence and . . ." She fell silent in the face of his renewed anger.

"Blast and blast and blast! I don't want to go to Almack's! I hate Almack's. And I won't attend some stupid evening listening to sopranos caterwauling or men torturing the strings of innocent violins! I tell you to your face, Charity Morris, I won't do it!"

"But Timon, you don't have to. Lady Heatherton will pick me up and take me to Lady Jersey's."

"And how will that look?"

Charity frowned. "Look? What do you mean, Timon?"

"If I do *not* take you? It will make me look a complete knave, that's what." He scowled at her fading color and saw the moment she made the decision that she'd *not* go. "Oh very well," he interjected quickly. "I *will* go. But I won't stay past the first interval. You must tell your Lady Heatherton she is to bring you home, is that clear?"

Charity's eyes lit up. "Oh, Timon, you will? Thank you. It will be a terrible sacrifice on your part and I want you to know I appreciate it. Very much, Timon"—she approached and laid her hand on his arm, looking up at him with her huge eyes—"you are truly a wonderful, generous man."

Timon growled, shook her off, and stomped off. "Just send Lady Heatherton a note."

He slammed the door and then, moments later, slammed the front door as well. "Wonderful man! How can she say anything so stupid when I've treated her . . ." He shut his mouth, only to open it to say in nonchalant tones, "Oh. Hello there, Robin." He recalled that Robin had taken his wife to the park and the scowl returned. "What do you mean by it, then?" he asked, and crawled up into the carriage.

Robin had noticed Timon's quick departure from the park. He knew his friend well and had patiently waited for him, expecting him to come storming out exactly as he had done. "Mean by it?" he asked when he'd given the pair the office to start. "Mean by what?"

"By taking my wife for a drive in the park, of course. And introducing her to every rake in town."

"If you'd do it yourself I wouldn't have to, would I? Not that it was an onerous duty, of course. Your little Charity is a delightful companion with a marvelous sense of humor. I like her."

Timon, growling, finally remembered that he rather liked her, too. It was just that it was impossible to remember it when he felt so angry. Unfortunately, ever since their fathers had announced they were to wed, he'd been angry a great deal of the time!

Charity joined Timon for breakfast the morning after Lady Jersey's musicale. "I wish to thank you again, Timon," she said, smiling rather shyly. "I enjoyed myself a great deal, and, although the soprano did rather squeal a bit on the high notes, I don't think the man playing his violin could be said to have tortured the strings, do you?"

Timon grimaced. Then, glancing up from his paper and seeing Charity's hopeful look, he grinned. "The soprano squealed a great deal. I didn't really listen to the violin player because I found a friend and we managed to sneak out for a game of piquet."

"I wondered where you'd gone. Thank you for remembering to return to take me in for refreshments before you said your good-byes! After the interval a flautist played and a harpist and then a pianist. I like the harp best. Do you think I could learn to play one?"

"You wouldn't like it," said Timon dismissively. The last thing he needed was to come home and find his wife practicing at a harp! "Only angels should play harps," he concluded. He eyed her, remembering a scene from when they were both much younger.

She met his gaze and tried very hard not to giggle. Timon chuckled softly, his gaze softening.

Speaking together they chanted, *"And you'ns will never be angels, no how, no way."*

They'd been enjoying nearly ripe apples, knowing they'd very likely suffer tummy aches later, when they were discovered by Lord Trenton's head gardener. The man had chased them out of the orchard, ranting at them as he waved his hoe dangerously near their heads. The line they both remembered had been the usually taciturn man's final words on the subject.

For the first time since they'd come to town, Timon left the house, very much in charity with Charity.

"Almack's," breathed Charity softly, looking around.

Robin chuckled, but Timon, wishing he were elsewhere, told her not to act the greenhead. He managed to greet

Lady Jersey in something approaching a socially acceptable manner, but when beyond that lady's sensitive hearing, wondered why the devil she couldn't keep a still tongue in her mouth.

"What's the matter, Tim," teased Robin. "She said nothing but the truth!"

"But it wasn't kind of her to bam Timon that way. It isn't merely because of me that he's appeared here. I know it isn't."

Tim grinned. "Well, there you're out! It is only because of you I'm here. As you must know, I detest Almack's, although I'd not dare say that anywhere near a patroness! But I'm here, and I suppose we'd better dance. Come along, Cherry."

Tim might protest that there was nothing more dreary than a country dance, but he was athletic and graceful, and Charity loved dancing with him. She glowed, drawing eyes. Her expression when she looked at Timon and his grin when he looked back did more to negate the gossip about the pair than anything else either could have done or said.

Timon agreed the dance had been fun and, carelessly, introduced her to one of his friends, and then another and even remembered Charity wasn't to waltz until she'd been approved for it so that he scowled when another buck approached, obviously hoping to gain the hand of the *ton*'s newest beauty for just that purpose. In lofty tones, he told the man to take himself off.

Eventually he took Charity onto the floor for one more dance, realizing too late that it was one of the newly introduced cotillions and that she didn't know the steps. He instantly took her off again, returning to the floor when another country dance was announced. And then, very tactfully for him, Timon turned Charity over to Lady Heatherton's care and made his escape.

* * *

After seeing her embarrassment at Almack's when she discovered she didn't know the latest dances Timon had something else to feel guilty about, but this time he didn't berate his wife for her lack. Instead, he hired a dancing master for her, announcing in a high-handed manner that she must remain home the next few mornings to receive the man.

Charity was both pleased that he'd thought of it and angry that he sounded so much like his father when informing her of it. And so she told him.

"I don't sound like him," he insisted.

"You do. Exactly like him."

"Never!" But there was a touch of a question, a hint of horror, in his staring eyes.

"Timon, you *did*."

He sighed. "Well then, it's all your fault," he said, *almost* admitting to the fault.

"It is?"

"If you didn't always look at me with those great big eyes and make me feel like I'm about two inches high I wouldn't yell at you."

"You didn't exactly yell, Timon, and"—she suddenly looked very much as if she might cry—"I truly don't want to make you feel two inches high."

"If I didn't yell, what did I do?"

Her tears faded. "You put your nose"—she demonstrated—"in the air and made a pronouncement. Cold as ice."

Timon rolled his eyes. After a moment he glanced at her, discovered she was, once again, watching him closely. "Charity, I give you permission to kick me whenever you think I'm acting like my father."

She clapped her hands over her mouth and her eyes sparkled, obviously at some sudden thought.

The look drew a quiver to his lips as he almost smiled in response. "Now what, Cherry?"

"But Timon, I wouldn't dare. You'd be quite black-and-blue if I did so *every time* you acted like your father!"

He sobered, the look of horror returning. "I *can't* be that bad."

"Yes, you can."

"Really?"

"Truly."

He ran fingers through his carefully "windswept" hairstyle, ruining his valet's work. Very quietly he said, "I don't want to be like him, Cherry. He made our young lives difficult, and his latest start has turned me into an ogre, but, really, truly, *I don't want to be like him.*" He drew in a deep breath and let it out slowly. "I'll try to do better."

"I'll only kick you when you are very very bad," she said soberly. But her eyes twinkled. "And Timon?"

"Yes?"

"I'm glad you hired a dancing master for me. I was a little worried. About attending the ball . . . ?"

He grinned and let out a mock sigh of relief, mopping nonexistent sweat from his brow. "Well, that's all right then?"

Once again, this time whistling cheerfully, he left the house much in charity with Charity.

That the Montmorency estate was situated out of town, somewhat west of Chelsea, meant the young couple was forced to eat an early dinner. Timon was not pleased. Nor was he pleased, as he had ever right to be, at his wife's looks. Charity entered the salon before dinner, dressed in her ball gown, her hair done up in the very latest style, and her eyes glowing in that way they had when she anticipated pleasure.

She looked good enough to eat, and Timon had a sudden vision of a dozen of the wilder town bucks laying siege to her. He scowled.

Charity, aware of his every mood, instantly sobered. Worried that something was wrong with her gown, she glanced down. Had she got a spot on it? Or crushed it? Or . . .

"There is nothing wrong with your gown," he said, his voice cold as ice.

Charity, her mouth set in a firm line, marched across the room . . .

. . . and kicked him.

His hand clutching his shin, he bent a pained look her way. "Why did you do that?"

"You told me to."

"I never did anything so—" Even as he spoke his eyes widened. "—stupid . . . Oh. Did I sound like *him* again?"

"Yes. But, Timon, if there is nothing wrong with my gown, what *is* wrong?"

"You're looking very lovely, Cherry," he said slowly.

She brightened. "I am?"

"Very."

For once Charity missed the dryness and only heard what she wished to hear. "Oh, I am so glad you like the gown. It is the nicest I've ever owned, you know. By far."

Timon was still musing over her words after dinner as he watched a footman settle her cloak around her shoulders. He led her out to the carriage. "You, know, Cherry, this *shouldn't* have been your first nice gown. You *should* have had a come-out and all the pretties girls are given on that occasion. Your father . . ."

Charity settled herself, careful of creasing her skirts. She sighed. "I don't quite know how it is, Timon, but Father doesn't have the money one needs for a presentation.

Although he explained it to me, I admit I didn't listen very closely. I had so hoped to come to my aunt here in London when I reached the proper age. I dreamed of it—'' What she'd dreamed of was being where Timon was! "—but then she went to Naples, so I couldn't have done so, anyway. I suppose he isn't a rich man . . . Timon?'' she asked when she finally noted he was shaking his head from side to side.

"Your father's an old screw. He's got a bee in his bonnet about not spending his money and, besides, he doesn't like London. He could well afford to hire a house for a season and, if your aunt wasn't available, he could have found a woman to present you, but that would have forced him to put himself out. In his way, Cherry, he's as cold and selfish as my father. He just *pretends* he isn't that way.''

"I know he isn't a *warm* man, but I don't think anyone *could be* as cold as your father, Timon!''

Timon, lounging on the forward seat, grinned. "You couldn't be more right about *that!* But''—his smile faded—"in a sort of way, your father is a far more selfish man than mine. Mine saw to it that, when I came up to town, my feet were set on the proper path. One could say, I suppose, that he did it so I'd not embarrass him by falling into the sort of scrapes greenheads get into, but I didn't get that impression. I think he didn't want me embarrassing *myself*—if you know what I mean?''

"I know. I suppose I should feel lucky mine found me such a sensible governess, although I don't think *he* saw her that way.''

Timon remembered the tall gaunt woman who had had Charity in charge for several years. "It was she who taught you about getting on in the *ton?*''

"Yes. Father set her the lessons she was to give me. She had to work the sort of lessons *she* thought I needed in and around what *he* wanted me taught. I learned how to pour tea properly and the proper depth to curtsy for different people. And she made me study the peerage, learning who had precedence, so that, if I ever had to design formal seating for a dinner, I'd know how to go about it and . . .''

"And all those boring bits girls have to learn," he interrupted, "including the fact one doesn't run all over London without a footman in tow!"

Charity giggled and Timon chuckled and, as the carriage rolled along the macadamized road, they remembered all sorts of things they could laugh about. Timon, when they rolled into the Montmorency drive, was *very much* in charity with Charity. Quite enough so that, when he heard her gasp and saw what it was she looked at, he told their coachman he was to slow down as he approached each of the illuminations set along the lane to the mansion.

"Oh Timon, look at that one!"

"That one" portrayed a nesting bird, her mate sitting on a branch singing. In fact each and every one of the illuminations had a lovebird theme.

"I have just remembered," said Charity when they'd stared their fill at the fourth one. "St. Valentine's Day is supposed to be when birds choose their mates."

Timon ignored her comment. "I wonder," he said, "how Lady Montmorency dared set lighted lamps along the road this way. What if the wind blew something over and a fire started."

"Oh, but just look, Timon, each illumination is like a little house. Don't you think some poor servant is sitting inside, shivering, making certain something of the sort does *not* happen?"

"Ah! Very likely that's it. Except . . . with that powerful lamp, and as small as those structures are, he may not be shivering. He may be too hot!"

They laughed some more as the carriage pulled up in front of the house. The door stood wide, and extra footmen stood by to help arriving guests from their carriages. Timon waved them away, handing down his wife himself and, putting her hand on his arm, led her inside. The large entrance hall was not overly full of guests, but there were more than a handful milling around, removing warm garments and greeting friends.

Above their heads a newly cleaned chandelier glittered and gleamed, shedding golden light on those below, making the women's jewels echo back their own gleam and glitter. Timon, removing Charity's cloak, froze. He stared at one of the matrons whose neck and arms appeared weighted down with gems which should have sparkled more than they did. They, unlike the chandelier, had not been recently cleaned! A young girl turned, and a double strand of pearls shed a rosy iridescence on the chit's skin, and earbobs swung with her every movement. Another matron, much younger than the first, held her head high to show the inch-wide band of sapphires around her neck, a delicate chain falling from that and ending with another, larger, sapphire resting on a bare expanse of chest.

Everywhere Timon looked, the women sported their best jewels. Once again guilt flooded into him. Why, he berated himself, had he forgotten Charity would need jewels? How could he have been such a fool? He handed her cloak to a waiting footman and, his hand biting into her arm, led Charity to the stairs, marching up them, his scowl well in place.

There was a receiving line at the top. Lord and Lady Montmorency were introducing Lord Montmorency's half sister. Lady Montmorency's brother, Sir James, hovered nearby and, with him, that odd Scottish doctor, Mr. Macalister, who spent a great deal of his time in the hospitals.

Dr. Mac, as he was called by many who knew him, studied young Lord Crandle's black-as-thunder brow. It was rumored the scamp was disenchanted with his wife, but, if the worried look she cast up at him was anything to judge by, she didn't feel the same. Dr. Mac lifted his hand, an involuntary desire to stop the young man, when, with only a growled word or two to his wife, Crandle stomped off, leaving his young wife staring after him.

"Well, noo, I think that purr damsel requirrres immediate rrrescue," Macalister murmured, rolling his rrrs in the way he did only when disturbed.

Mac left his friend's side to approach the chit. "We've not been introduced Lady Crandle, but I know Lord Trrrenton rrrather well. If you will trust me," said Macalister, his soft Scottish tongue emphasizing the kindness in his eyes, "I will noo escort you to the ballroom, where you may find your frrriends?"

Macalister gave Charity one of his most reassuring smiles, but it faded quickly when, his kindness tearing down the barriers, tears welled up in her glorious eyes.

Instantly he whisked her into an empty parlor. Mac left the door ajar, as was proper, but led Lady Crandle to chairs off to the side, where they'd not be noticed by anyone passing by. Silently he handed her a snowy white handkerchief and then, patiently, he waited.

"I'm so—" She hiccoughed. "—sorry. Truly, I'm not usually such a water—" *Hic.* "—watering pot."

"That husband of yours deserves to be shot."

"Oh no." Clutching the handkerchief in both hands, Charity stared earnestly at her rescuer. "It isn't *his* fault. You see, he didn't wish to wed me." Charity frowned. "Or, perhaps, it is that he didn't wish to wed just yet?"

"Och! Then he did expect to marry you?" asked Macalister, intrigued. "Eventually?"

"Well, he always said, oh from when we were *quite* young,

that one day we'd wed. It's just that he didn't quite like it just at the moment, I think.''

"Tell me.''

So Charity did.

Except for Lady Heatherton, Charity had talked of her problem to no one. Macalister's sympathy and concern touched her deeply, and she found herself pouring out the whole story, beginning with how Timon and she had become friends at an early age and how they'd had adventures and how, when Timon got older, she didn't see so much of him, but they still rode together when he was home and he'd tell her all he was doing and all about his races and his new horses and his friends and their adventures.

''. . . But then''—she drew in a deep wavering breath—''our fathers got this silly notion into their heads.''

"And they weren't particularly tactful about informing you of it?'' asked Macalister when it appeared she'd finished. Macalister didn't know Charity's father, but he knew Lord Trenton!

She smiled a glimmering of a smile. *"Not at all tactful.* In fact, we'd neither of us a hint of what was in the wind when we were ordered into Lord Trenton's library and informed the announcement was to be made immediately and the wedding as soon as the banns had been called! Timon . . .'' Again her voice trailed off before she finished.

"Lord Crandle wasn't pleased.''

She stared at him, her eyes wide and innocent. "Surely no man wishes to be told who and when he is to marry?''

"Such marrrriages were once common. It is only recently parents have been more generous in allowing their offspring a say in the matter.''

"Truly?''

"Truly.''

Charity thought about that. "Still, I don't think that

changes anything. Poor Timon wasn't ready to wed and settle down. Worse, his father expected us to live not far from Trenton Hall. That really upset Timon. He married me as ordered, but absolutely refused to live in the country."

"Hmmm . . ." Macalister rubbed his chin, wondering if he should explain what he knew.

While he mused, she did, too. "I've wondered . . ." she said softly, but then stopped.

"You've wondered, Lady Crandle?"

"Well"—she peered up at the doctor, wondering if he could tell her—"sometimes I've thought Lord Trenton isn't *quite* as well as one would like, and that might explain it? He hasn't *said* anything. Not that he *would,* of course. Admitting to any weakness would be . . . would be . . ."

"Would be very unlike him," Macalister finished tactfully.

"Yes. You do know Lord Trenton, do you not?"

Macalister thought of the blunt words he'd used not six months earlier when telling his lordship just how badly his lordship's health had deteriorated. He'd told Lord Trenton he must cut back, not work so hard, must take time to relax, rest more . . .

"Doctor?"

"Hmm? Oh yes. I know Lord Trenton. He is a verrra stubborn man."

Charity giggled. "I don't believe there is a more stubborn man anywhere—unless it is Timon!" She got a sad look when she mentioned her husband.

Macalister made a guess: "I think you love the lad . . . ?"

"Oh, since *forever,* "said Charity, not hesitating a moment when admitting it.

"And does your Timon know that?"

"Yes . . ." She cast Macalister a startled look. "Well . . . maybe not?—" The look turned thoughtful. "—I haven't a notion," she finished, frowning. "I just always assumed he must know . . ."

"A man rrrarely just *knows,* my lady," said Macalister, smiling. He studied young Lady Crandle, who was rapidly pulling herself back together, and plotted ways of setting the young couple straight. When the doctor was certain Lady Crandle had recovered her spirits, he suggested he take her to the ballroom.

Crandle, from all Macalister had ever heard, was not a bad lad. He was young and self-centered, but those failings could be laid at the feet of most young men, and time would heal the "sickness" which was called youth. Nevertheless, the cure would proceed more quickly if a dose of reality was forced down the lad's throat!

Rather smugly, Macalister justified his decision to interfere with Lord and Lady Crandle: As Lord Trenton's doctor, Macalister was obliged, was he not, to do what he could for his patient—especially when the patient would not do it for himself! Lord Trenton needed his son's help if he was to survive. With rest and no worries, Lord Trenton could live a normal life span.

But if he did *not* give over his current tension-filled way of living, with all the responsibilities of a great estate and an active political life, he could die at any moment.

And so young Crandle would know before this evening ended!

Besides, the young fool was blessed with a lovely, generous, young beauty of a wife. So perhaps it was also a good notion to tell the boy a few home truths about a woman's emotions as well . . . ? It was time, thought Macalister, glancing at one of the many cupids with which Lady Montmorency had decorated the ballroom, that someone gave the god of love a hand!

Eros, thought Macalister, using Cupid's Greek name, *is playing this particular game without a full deck. I'll just see if I*

*can't pass him an ace or two to fill out his hand—and then raise
the ante a bit!*

One of the first women Lady Crandle saw upon entering
the ballroom was Lady Heatherton. She thanked Mr.
Macalister for his kindness and told him she'd be quite all
right now.

He watched her join her friend, saw how pleased that
lady was to see Charity, and retired to the wall to watch
and plot ways and means. The first thing he saw was Lord
Crandle waltzing by with one of the *ton*'s more talked-
about widows on his arm. Macalister's brow arched, and
he turned his glance toward Lady Crandle . . . who obviously knew about the fast widow's reputation. The glowing
smile with which Lady Crandle had joined Lady Heatherton had faded, and her pretty lips drooped.

"Unless you want Lady Montmorency to introduce you,
willy-nilly, to the ugliest wallflower warming a chair, you'd
better come with me and disappear into the card room,"
said a soft voice filled with humor.

Macalister turned, an idea rapidly taking form at the
sound of the well-known voice. Sir Ivor Cottersbourne.

"Damn my eyes, if it isn't London's foremost rake. Sir
Ivor, you are *just* the man we need."

"Me?" said his lordship ungrammatically.

"You," said Dr. Mac happily. "I couldn't have come up
with a better cat's-paw if I'd searched m'mind for hours!"

Ivor's smile faded. "Cat's-paw, is it? Mac, I don't think
I like the sound of this . . ."

"Nonsense, mon! You need only act yourself."

"Are you certain you've the right person?"

"With your slightly blighted reputation, you are *just* the
one to flirt a trifle with Lady Crandle."

Cottersbourne blinked. "Do what? With whom?"

Mac laughed the low rumbling laugh that was so infectious. "Come along now, m'brawny mon, and we'll just have a wee talk about it all." He led his friend into an alcove. "First off, have ye heard the gossip about Crandle?"

"Recently married but still acting like a man free from shackles," said the baronet promptly.

"Hmm. Exactly. And little Lady Crandle suffers for it." Macalister gestured toward he dancers. "Just look at the silly lad!"

The *lad* was gazing raptly into the little widow's eyes, his mouth quirked in the faintest of leering smiles.

"That one will eat him alive," said Cottersbourne dryly.

"He's too green to know that. Besides, he doesn't *rrreally* wish to seduce the widow. The silly chub really wishes to seduce his wife."

"And how, my good doctor, does one go about diagnosing *that* particular malady . . . to say nothing of what I'm guessing you think will be a cure?"

"He needs waking up, is all."

"Waking up." Cottersbourne eyed Mac with a jaundiced eye. "Which you think I can do?"

"Of course. All you need do, laddy, is appear to have developed a sudden tendre for his wife, and our young fool'll be like a dog with a bone."

"Ah! So"—Cottersbourne's brows arched—"when he demands satisfaction I'm to allow him to blow a hole in me? He is an excellent shot, in case you didn't know."

"Och mon, it won't go so far as that. Ye give him reason to think a reputed rake is interested in his wife, and he'll trot to her side on the instant. And, given the choice, his wife will choose him."

"Mac, you're mistaken. It won't work that way."

"Of course it will. Don't fail me, Ivor. You're my ace in the hole."

"Ace? More like the knave of hearts, given what you ask of me!"

"I'm asking that you pretend, *and that you only pretend,* an interest in a very nice young lady. You won't find it difficult. She looks very well in her new feathers."

Ivor knew his friend. Mac wouldn't give up, but would keep on and on and on until he gave in. He sighed. "So, point out this paragon to me."

Mac did and Ivor's brows rose. "Crandle is fool enough to take up with the Black Widow when he's got *that* at home?"

"It's a case of cutting off the nose to spite the face. He's merely rebelling to get even with his father and forgetting how much he really likes the wife who suffers for it."

"Oh, very good, Mac! Not only am I to rouse his jealousy, but it will be spiked by the guilt he is very likely feeling. Mac, when I lie dead at your feet, I hope you are satisfied."

"Ye'll do it?"

Ivor scowled. "I don't like the widow. I will do what I can to see the lad doesn't fall under her evil spell."

"You say that as if you've experience . . . ?"

"A cousin committed suicide. She was named in his will."

"No!"

"She's like a spider spinning webs and entangling the feet of the young. She doesn't care a rap for any of them, Mac, just that they fall under her spell."

"Ivor," said Macalister earnestly, "I beg you. Not only for the little lady, but for the man she loves, play Cupid for me!"

"I'll be the oddest Cupid ever, will I not?" Ivor chuckled. Sobering, he studied Charity, was struck by her pert little face, saw her eyes sparkle at something Lady Heatherton said, and was reconciled. "Introduce me, Mac."

"I think not," said Mac.

"First you will and then you won't?" asked Ivor, shaking his head.

"*Instead* I'll get *Lady Jersey* to introduce you."

"Sir Ivor, you are flirting with me," accused Charity, a glower lowering her brows over the eyes she raised to glare him.

"Won't you forget the sir and just call me Ivor?" he asked in a low, teasing voice.

"I don't believe I will," she said slowly. "Lady Jersey said you were a bit of a rogue. It is quite easy to believe," she scolded.

"Ah, but only a bit of a rouge, you will recall. Not a fully fledged raptor pushed out of the nest by its parents!" He nodded to where a medallion hung with ribbons and a golden cupid showed a pair of cooing birds seated on a silver branch.

Charity instantly grabbed what appeared an innocuous topic of conversation. "Lady Montmorency has provided lovely decorations, has she not?" she asked primly.

Ivor chuckled. "If I *were* flirting with you, my lady, you would do your best to stop it, would you not?" He glanced to the side where Lord Crandle, along with a few other young bucks, surrounded the beguiling widow. "Perhaps you should take lessons from that lady."

"I think not," said Charity with more ice than one usually heard in her low tones.

"I compliment you."

She blinked and glanced up at her partner to find that, for once, he wasn't smiling down at her. "Compliment me?"

A muscle jumped in his jaw. "You are very wise that you'll not take that succubus as a model."

Charity frowned. "Succubus . . . but is that not a . . . a female demon?"

One of Ivor's brows arched that she knew the word. "A demon in female form, is, I believe the proper definition."

"Which is not *quite* the same thing . . ." Charity cast a worried look toward her husband. "Why do you call her a demon?"

The muscle jumped again. " She casts spells over men like the sirens of old. I do not wish to talk of her." Ivor forced a smile. "I'd much rather talk about those great glowing eyes that look at one in such a way one wishes to drown in them. Or about your lovely skin that glows as if it were dusted with powdered pearls. Or about your hair, which gleams with health and asks a man to pull out the pins and combs holding it high on your head so that it may fall around you . . . and around him when he—"

Perforce he stopped when Charity placed her fingers over his lips. She felt him place a kiss there and blushed rosily. Just then their steps took them near the chair where the widow sat, and Charity looked straight into her husband's glowering eyes. She looked away, blushing more deeply.

When she dared to look that way again, Timon stood a little apart from the widow, his arms crossed, never taking his eyes from herself.

"Oh dear," she murmured.

"I would very much like to be your dear," said Ivor, chuckling softly. "But why," he asked, "do I suspect it is not I to whom you refer?"

"Hmm? Oh! Do stop your flirting, Sir Ivor! This is terrible. I am a married lady, and this is not at all proper behavior."

"No. You *should* be flirting with your husband, should you not?" He watched a tide of rosy color rise again into her cheeks. "I wonder why he is such a fool. If you were my wife, you'd not have to watch *me* flirting elsewhere."

Charity sighed. "Again, Sir Ivor, I must tell you you are not behaving properly."

"But my dear, that is the whole point. I am *ordered* to, er, misbehave. I have been sent on a rescue mission, you see."

She frowned. "Rescue mission?" she asked cautiously.

"You perceive in me an ace up Cupid's sleeve, my dear."

"That sounds rather underhanded," she said sternly. "It is surely against every rule of gambling to have a card up one sleeve! And how can you be part of a deck of cards, anyway?"

"It has been suggested the deck should be tampered with." Ivor grinned. "I am merely to make your husband jealous."

"Jealous?" she asked even more warily.

"Our mutual friend Macalister has made a plot," he confided. "He's a very odd-looking Cupid, of course, that great burly Scotsman!"

"Mutual friend? But I only met Mr. Macalister this evening."

"And he instantly took you under his wing! Yes, very like our Dr. Mac."

"Please, will you explain to me what you mean?"

"When you look at me with those great huge innocent eyes I will do anything you ask of me," he said, fervently . . . and discovered he actually meant it. He sighed softly, glanced to where Dr. Mac stood watching them, sent a brief glower that way, then looked back at the young bride. "My lady, it is simple. Your husband needs to see what he has and must learn to value it properly. So long as you sit to the side and let him go his way he will continue running off in all directions except the one direction he should go."

"I do not wish to do anything which will anger Timon. I love him too much to hurt him. You must stop this game you play. Instantly."

"But, my lady," said Ivor, wide-eyed, "Cupid has demanded you and your Timon come to terms and has chosen me as his emissary. I cannot give it over!"

"You don't understand. Timon has . . . has been showing every sign he is coming out of his tantrum, and I truly believe that if I am very careful, he will remember he loves me and that, soon, everything will be quite all right again, do you not see?"

"If he is coming around, then a prick to his conscience should make everything right still sooner."

"Oh no! It is his *conscience* which has kept things *wrong* for so long! He hates admitting he is in the wrong!"

"You appear to know him very well."

"Oh, I *do,*" said Charity earnestly. "He and I have been friends since we were children. I know him, all his good points . . . and, of course"—she sighed softly—"his bad as well. He is a *very* stubborn man."

The music stopped just then and, as Sir Ivor had planned, they were very near to where Macalister stood watching. "Since I cannot make you understand, my lady, will you talk to Dr. Mac? It is his plan, after all."

"He . . . was very kind to me," she said, doubtfully.

"Then doesn't he deserve a hearing?" asked Sir Ivor.

Macalister's ears were very good and, as he'd been meant to do, he overheard the exchange. Seeing that another push to the plot was needed, he stepped forward.

"My lady," said Dr. Mac, "if you would be kind eough to go along to the garden room with Sir Ivor, I will find refreshments for the three of us and bring a tray there." Macalister looked toward where Lord Crandle was making a determined way toward where they stood. "It won't take

me more than a minute or two . . . and then I'll explain
everything."

"Very well," said Charity, not absolutely certain she
should agree. "The garden room?" She looked from one
to the other.

"Just along the hall to the back. The door may be shut,
noo, but go on in. It is a very pleasant room," said the
doctor, who had had a patient occupying it during most
of each day for the past few weeks.

Sir Ivor offered his arm, and Charity, after another brief
hesitation, laid her fingers on it. As the couple moved out
the door, Macalister moved to intercept Timon. It would
not do to allow the young man to follow too quickly. Not
that, when he did, there would be anything to see, but he
must be allowed to think there might be for the time it
would take for him to remember he loved his wife . . .

. . . assuming he did, of course. Macalister realized that
was something he did not know. He had only Lady Crandle's word that Lord Crandle had expected to wed her
eventually . . . and his behavior when he'd noticed Ivor
dancing with her. Macalister relaxed. The lad's behavior
might be merely dog-in-the-mangerish, but then again, it
might be full-fledged jealousy.

Macalister hunted through his mind for what he knew
of the young man, searching for a means of delaying him.
Aha, he thought. "Lord Crandle," said Mac. "I have heard
it said you are an excellent instructor for men needing
help with their driving."

"Not now." Timon tried to peer around the big Scot.
"Sorry . . . must . . ."

But Mac had no notion of cooperating. He took Timon's
arm in his huge paw and turned him toward the convenient
alcove to which he'd previously taken Ivor. "Now, then, I
admit to you I'm the merest whipster, but, I need to get
around London, so it's important I improve . . ."

"Sir, I don't believe I know you. At the moment," Timon added, rudely, "I don't want to know you. Excuse me." Pulling free, he turned on his heel and escaped.

Macalister sighed and, following along behind, trailed Timon into the hall, where the lad looked in both directions. "I don't suppose . . ."

"Unless you can tell me where to find my wife, I have nothing to say to you," said Timon.

"If you tell me *why* you want to find your wife, perhaps I can help you," said Macalister, quietly.

Timon, about to head off in the wrong direction, stopped. Very slowly he turned. "What do you know about my wife?"

"I know she is a very unhappy young lady being treated in a scoundrelly fashion by a young man who purports to love her."

"I have nev . . ." Timon sighed. "I suppose I have told her that. Years ago." He pokered up. "Not that it is any of *your* business . . ."

"I have made it my business."

Timon blinked and climbed, again, onto his high horse! "Of all the . . ."

Macalister bowed, which stopped Timon's incipient rant. He tried again. "It is outside of enough that you . . ."

But, when Mac merely bowed agreement, once again Timon's voice trailed off.

Timon drew in a deep breath. "What right do you think you have to interfere between a man and his wife?" Timon's voice, which had been getting louder, was, this time, dangerously controlled.

"The right of a doctor worried about his patient," said Macalister promptly.

"My wife . . ."

". . . is not my patient."

Timon's brows lowered slightly and so did his voice. "Not . . . my wife."

"No."

"My . . . father?"

"Well, noo! The lad has a brain or two between his ears," said Macalister, his eyes trained on the ceiling. "One had begun to wonder . . ."

Timon ignored the insult, interrupting to demand, "What is wrong with my father?"

"He's a verra sick man, that's what's wrong with him," said Macalister sternly.

"He hasn't said a word . . ." Timon's anger collapsed, and he seemed to shrink with it. "But he wouldn't, of course."

"Oh, well, noo, he's not a man to complain, of course," agreed Macalister.

"Blast."

"Exactly."

"My wife . . ." Timon recalled why he was looking for his wife. "That rake! Where has he taken her? She's an innocent, you know. She hasn't a notion of the tricks a man like that can get up to. She'll . . ." Timon's eyes widened in horror. "Macalister, if you know where they've gone, tell me. At once."

"I'll take you there if you'll not go a'tearrring in like a madman demanding the villain unhand the lass!"

"And why should I not?"

"Because they are expecting me at any moment. I promised to arrive with refreshments. I can't see Ivor seducing a young lady when a third person is about to come in on him."

Timon, as Macalister had discovered, had a brain. He drew in a deep breath. "You set this up. You interfering . . . !"

"Laddie, did someone not need to interfere?" asked Macalister quietly.

Timon couldn't hold the Scot's gaze. His eyes fell. "You don't know . . ."

"Don't I? I have known your father for a donkey's years, lad. I know verra well the Cliffe temper and the Cliffe stubbornness. You have it in full measure, do you not?" Macalister grimaced. "But, laddie, it is not your stubbornness which is important here. It's your father. The old fool will kill himself before he'll admit to you he needs your help to remain among the living."

"Truly?" asked Timon after a moment. "He is in such very bad shape?"

"I fear he is."

Timon sighed. "Will you please take me to my wife?"

Macalister remembered Ivor's half-jocular demand that he'd be sorry when the duel was over! "Have I your promise . . . ?"

"That I'll not cause a scene? So long as you are correct, and, in strictest propriety, they merely await you, then there will be no reason for me to cause a scene, will there?"

Macalister remembered the temptation he'd felt to take the sobbing Lady Crandle into his arms and console her. Would the chit have, again, succumbed to her unhappiness? "I can think of one circumstances where what you might see could be misinterpreted . . ."

Timon's lips compressed. "Take me to my wife."

"So be it."

Macalister led Timon toward the garden room. He was unsurprised to find the door shut tightly but sighed at such lack of self-preservation on the part of Cottersburne. He wished he could peek into the room, could give some warning they were coming, could do something which would guarantee the two would be seated in individual chairs and some distance from each other.

The doctor opened the door.

"Damn you!" said Timon, staring.

"Thank God!" said a distracted Sir Ivor, glancing in their direction. "Mac, you must . . ."

"Hush now," said Mac, soothingly. He gently turned Charity away from Sir Ivor. "Lady Crandle, m'lass . . ."

Charity, her face wet with tears, looked up. "Oh, Dr. Mac, I can't—" She looked around. "—Timon . . . ?" She struggled free, and wiped her cheeks with her hands. "Oh dear, Timon . . . !"

"Yes. Timon. Your *husband*, Charity Morris!"

Charity's back firmed into a poker-straight line. "Charity Cliffe, Lord Crandle. *For the very last time*, my name is Charity Cliffe. You will *not* forget it again."

"Assuming *you* do not! How dare you allow that man, that *rake*, to hug you?"

"The poor man was not hugging me. He was comforting me."

"Ha! He's a rake. He'd use any excuse . . ."

"You, my lord," said Ivor in as cold a tone as Lord Trenton had ever used, "are either a born fool or you don't know your wife at all or you don't care. And whatever the case, I've every intention of teaching you your manners!"

Timon opened his mouth to respond and closed it. "Are you giving me a challenge?" he asked, astounded.

Ivor laughed harshly. "I guess I am."

"Now isn't that a turnabout! You, the rake, challenging his lover's husband?"

"You see? You no more know your wife than you know a red Indian!"

"I know Cherry very well indeed. And if you ever lay another hand to her, I'll take up that challenge and, if you survive, I'll offer one of my own! Cherry . . ." Timon turned to her. "Cherry, we have to go home. Now."

"Home?"

He came to her, and his voice low, said, "I've been a fool Cherry. I never once asked myself *why* my father insisted I marry you."

A new worry pushing aside her own concerns, Cherry glanced toward Dr. Mac. "He . . . His . . . He isn't . . ."

"He's a verra sick man, my lady," said Macalister kindly.

"So that is . . . ?"

"That would explain it all," said Timon. "Our marriage. His insistence we live at Mumford Manor. Everything—" Timon let her go and paced the room. "Cherry, can you forgive me?"

"Tell him no," suggested Ivor, still with that dangerous note to his voice. He now leaned, arms crossed, against the mantel. "Then, in six months, if he's proved he's turned over a new leaf he might ask you again."

"You stay out of this," stormed Timon. "Cherry?"

"Home . . . you mean Mumford Manor?"

"I suppose I was thinking of Trenton Hall, but you are correct that we must go to the manor . . ."

"We cannot just *go*, Timon. We must make plans."

"My father . . ."

"But, Timon, I must organize the packing and see if any of the servants will come with us and . . . A day or two?"

"Hmm . . ." Timon glanced at Macalister, who nodded. "A day or two, then."

Timon held out his hand, and Cherry put hers into it. He pulled her close and, protectively, tucked her under his arm, his hand at her waist. "Mr. Macalister, thank you for telling me about m'father's health. I should have known, but I was far too angry . . ."

"Och noo, your father is much too stubborn to give you a hint. Don't fash yourself lad. You'll do now you've got your head on straight."

"And remember," said Ivor, his eyes narrowed, "that if you do *not*, you'll have me to answer to."

Timon's anger was roused by the baronet's tone. "You just keep your nose out of my business!"

"I would willingly, Lord Crandle," said Sir Ivor smoothly, "if I didn't feel driven to see to your wife's comfort and her future."

"And by what right to you think to interfere with my wife?"

"The right any man has," said Ivor quietly, "to see that a good woman is not mistreated by those who should have a care for her comfort."

Timon and Ivor stared at each other for a long moment. Charity laid her hand on her husband's and he glanced down at her, noted her worried look, and relaxed, grinning. "I see. Yes, I'll admit you've got that right. And I'll make damne"—he glanced at Charity—"*dashed* certain you never have cause to take care of this particular good woman!"

"See that you don't."

"Sir Ivor," said Charity quickly.

"Yes, my dear?"

"He really does love me, you know. And now he's remembered it, so you truly don't have to concern yourself."

"Just keep in mind that I'll happily come to your rescue anytime Cupid requires it of me." He grinned a quick slashing grin.

Charity smiled in return. "It is *not* proper to have aces up one's sleeve," she insisted.

"Cherry . . ." said Timon, unhappy with the rapport he felt between the two. "We really must go . . . ?"

"I'm coming." Charity freed herself and went to Dr. Mac. She reached up and tugged at his shoulders. When he leaned toward her she put a kiss on his cheek. "Thank you," she said softly, and turned to Sir Ivor. She held out her hand.

Ivor, a rueful look in his eyes, asked, "I don't get a kiss?"

"You know you don't. Timon would not understand, and we might be right back where we started."

Ivor took her hand and, holding it with both his, flicked a look toward Timon before raising it to place a kiss on her knuckles. "He doesn't deserve you."

"And you think you do?" asked Timon with only a little belligerence.

"No. I know I do not. I only wish I *were* deserving of someone so lovely who would be half so loyal and loving toward me as this woman is toward you." Ivor sighed and, for just a moment, revealed a sort of loneliness one didn't expect to see in a rake.

"Oh dear. Perhaps . . ." said Charity softly.

"No," said Timon firmly. He took his wife under his arm again, in that protective manner he'd used earlier and, with a nod to Macalister, a thoughtful look toward Ivor, he led her from the room. As he closed the door he said in that same firm tone, "Sir Ivor Cottersbourne is more than capable of solving his own problems, so don't you dare think you might . . . !"

The door shut with a snap and Sir Ivor, his mouth set in a wry twist, raised one brow and stared at Macalister.

Dr. Mac smiled. "I, too, think you could, if you would, solve your problem!"

For half a moment Sir Ivor wondered if Macalister had the least notion of exactly what his problem was!

"Cherry?" said Timon, when their carriage had passed down the lane and onto the river road on its way back toward Mayfair.

He sat beside her for the trip back into London, his arm

still around her. A long curl had fallen from under the hood to her cloak and lay against her breast. He could just touch it and did so, again and again, letting the tress curl around the end of his finger.

"Cherry?"

"Yes, Timon?"

"Can you forgive me?"

"No."

"No!"

She giggled. "I cannot forgive when I see no fault. I never blamed *you,* Timon."

"Did you not?" he mused. "Then why have I felt so guilty?"

"Because, perhaps, you blame yourself?"

"Hmm. Cherry, I always knew you were not at fault. I *knew* I was angry at m'father. Yet I could not get past it to see what a good thing he'd done for me."

"A good thing, Timon?"

"You knew I'd marry you, did you not? Someday. When I got around to it . . . ?" A touch of dry humor lightened his tone.

"Oh yes." She didn't smile or even look at him. "From when we were very young you said we'd wed. Someday."

"Hmm." Timon's forehead crinkled up. "I wonder if *someday* would have arrived if I had been left to my own devices . . . ?"

"Oh," said Charity in a very small voice.

"Don't be angry, Cherry," he said quickly. "I'm a selfish brute, I know that, but once someone has shown me my error, I usually see where I've gone wrong. Without thinking about it, I had it in my head you'd wait patiently, that when I was ready to settle down, there you'd be, ready as well. I know how thoughtless that was of me, but, Cherry . . . you always have waited."

"I've always been there when you wished me to be there.

I see. So it *is* my fault?" Rather severely, she added, "*Again?*"

For a long moment Timon was silent. "Am I doing it again?"

"I think you are. You are trying very hard to find reasons why you are not at fault, Timon, and I think I must not let you do it. It was very wrong of you to treat me so badly. It was no one but yourself who did it. You, yourself, alone."

Timon sighed. "Then you do not forgive me."

"I have already said there is nothing to forgive."

"But you just said . . . !"

"I don't feel it necessary to forgive you for treating me as you did, but I'll not forgive you for being so angry with your father you could not see straight!"

"I don't understand."

"Timon, I will forgive you for that when and if you will accept that *you yourself alone* are at fault and that there is no excuse, no one else you may blame—" After half a moment she added, "—and that you are sorry for it."

"You sound very unlike my Cherry," he said, turning slightly and picking up the curl with his other hand.

"I suppose I do, but I have realized something. I, too, have been wrong-headed, Timon," she said, and sighed.

"You have?"

"I have let you go on in your hurtful ways without ever once telling you you were hurting me. It is possible that, selfish as you are, you did not realize how badly you hurt me again and again?"

"Damn it, Cherry!"

"Well?"

He sighed. Tugging gently at the curl, he sighed again. "You will not allow me even the tiniest excuse? M'father . . . ?"

"Your father, Timon, is the man he's always been. I will not be happy if you turn into a man very like him!"

Horrified at the thought, Timon let her go. "I don't want that either!"

"But in one way, I wish you *were* like him."

"What?"

"Yes, in one way. He has always been the most responsible of men, doing the work of several, and never blaming anyone but himself when something is not done or goes wrong. My father has commented on it more than once."

"He takes responsibility for his actions, is that what you are saying?"

"Hmm. Timon, you have always been a very charming person. Even when you were very much a boy. You've been allowed to do as you would by far too many people, beginning with your nurse and the Trenton Hall cook and the head groom and . . . and me, too," she finished in a small voice.

For a moment Timon was silent. "Rob was saying only the other day that we were two spoiled brats who didn't wish to grow up and become adults. Is that what you are saying, too?"

Charity sighed. "Not just you, Timon. Me as well. I have tried to remain exactly as I always was, your little friend, grateful for any crumbs you let fall my way. That was childish, Timon. I mustn't be that way any longer."

"You mean you won't be grateful for crumbs?"

"Don't try to charm me, Timon, and don't laugh at me. You know exactly what I mean."

"I wonder where you learned to stand up for yourself . . . ?" He put his fingers over her mouth when she'd have spoken. "No, I don't mean that. I wonder when you learned to stand up for yourself all over again! You used to, and it was one of the things I liked about you. You *didn't* just say yes Timon, no Timon, God bless Timon! If you didn't agree, you'd tell me so. But then you didn't . . . You stopped . . ."

"I think it was when I realized I loved you that I changed."

Timon cast her a worried look, and took her back under his arm, cuddling her close. "Cherry, you aren't saying you've stopped loving me and that is why you've changed back? Are you? I know I don't deserve your love after treating you the way I did, but that's all over. We'll go to the manor and we'll . . ." His arm tightened and he glanced down at the top of her head, a sudden notion filling his mind to the exclusion of all else. "Hmmm, Cherry, do you think . . . ?"

Hidden from his eyes because she was looking down at her hands tightly clenched in her lap, Cherry smiled a tight little smile. Maybe all that work on the christening gown hadn't been wasted after all!

"Cherry?"

Timon tipped her face up to his. Very slowly he lowered his lips to hers. When she didn't object to that first gentle kiss, he did it again. Then, when her arms crept up around his neck, he pulled her tightly against him and kissed her thoroughly.

They were both more than a little mussed when the coach finally pulled up before their front door just off Hanover Square.

Two and a half years later!

Timon took another turn around the terrace at Trenton Hall, patting the back of his fussing son and then, when the boy would not stop his grizzling, handed the teething babe back to the nurse awaiting him.

"Why will Francis not stop crying?" he asked no one in particular.

"He is teething," soothed Charity, who, her body well rounded with their second child, sat back in a cane lounge chair watching her husband and her son with the loving smile which lit her face from the inside out.

"And why does Father not arrive? He said to expect him this morning, did he not? It is well past noon."

"Something has delayed him, Timon. A horse lost a shoe, perhaps. Do not add your fussing to that of our son," she said in a mock-scold sort of tone. *"You* must set Francis *a good example.* I know Lord Trenton has been gone almost since we arrived from London, but you cannot think anything is *wrong* with him. Why, his letters have sparkled with news of all he's seen and done!"

"Yes, but I want . . ." He turned a sideways look toward Charity who grinned at him. He grinned back. "You are right, of course, and I am being very foolish, I suppose."

"Once he's gone over the books he cannot help but approve the changes you've made, Timon."

"Do you think so?" asked Timon, with a touch of ruefulness. "Success was not always sufficient to justify the things I've done in the past!"

Charity chuckled. "Do not concern yourself, my love. He will be so enamored of his grandson, he'll not even notice you've begun growing those awful turnips."

"Do not *you* start in on my mangel-wurzels! I got enough of that nonsense from our land agent!"

"Until you took him to a meeting of the Society of Agriculture and made him read about the vegetable in Young's *Annals of Agriculture.* I believe you said that had him, grudgingly, willing to try them?"

"Yes, well, that was *your* idea, and I'd thank you for it except now the man wants to try every new thing that comes along!"

Charity laughed and reached her hands to her husband, who helped her to her feet. "Then anything your father disapproves, you can tell him what might have happened if you hadn't had control of things! I do believe he is finally coming. At least I think I heard a carriage . . . ?"

The couple, followed by the nurse carrying their son, turned the corner of the house and there, loaded with trunks and bandboxes and spattered with mud, was a great traveling carriage.

And, helping a spritely lady down the two steps to the ground, was Lord Trenton. A deeply tanned and laughing Lord Trenton.

Timon looked at Charity and Charity stared right back, and then, simultaneously realizing they were acting like a pair of noodles, they stepped forward.

It was only as they approached that Charity recognized the woman. "Aunt! Timon, it is my aunt. Welcome, Lord Trenton, Lady . . ."

She was interrupted by her smiling father-in-law. "You will, please, welcome the new Lady Trenton! We were married in Naples before we began our travels."

"Married . . ."

Again Charity and Timon looked at each other, this time with a slight frown marring each young brow.

"I told you we should inform our families," said Lady Trenton, "but you would have it the surprise would be good for them!" She chuckled, moving on light feet to her niece. "Charity, my love, you are glowing. And is that your son I see?" She moved to the nurse and took the child into her own arms. "Lucas, come meet your grandson," she called softly, her eyes never leaving the suddenly quiet child. "Why, Luke, my love, he looks just like you! He even has a frown."

"Now Maria, you know I lost my frown! I charge anyone to frown in the face of your smiles! Francis, my boy . . ." he finished softly, gently touching the toddler's downy cheek with one long finger. "Now, what do you mean he looks like me? I don't see why women always say a babe looks like this person or that person . . ."

Francis grabbed his grandfather's finger and would not let go.

"Why, I think he likes me," said Lord Trenton, sounding surprised.

"At the moment, my lord, he likes anyone who will pay him attention. He is teething, you see, and needs a great deal of distracting from his pain."

"Teething! Oh, you poor mite. Nurse, have you tried . . ." And Lady Trenton walked off with both the babe and the nurse, her voice trailing back to them as she catechized the nurse on her nursery practices.

Lord Trenton smiled after his wife. "She has always been a wonderful woman. I just didn't know how wonderful until we met again in Naples."

"You knew my aunt before, then?"

"Charity, I wanted to marry your aunt years and years ago, but . . . I was too slow in making up my mind. Not this time, however!" He smiled broadly. "I don't believe I'd been a week in Italy when I asked her to marry me."

"But you didn't think it news we'd appreciate having?" asked Timon, frowning.

"I . . ." Lord Trenton looked embarrassed. Then he straightened. "If it is any of your business, young man, I"—the red in his ears reached his cheeks—"was afraid to tell you," he finished in a rush.

"You . . . were *afraid?*"

"You are always so blasted disapproving," huffed the older man.

"*I* am disapproving!"

"Yes, you. You . . . frightened me half to death when I first saw you in your cradle and, well, it is stupid, I suppose, but I never got over it. . . ."

Charity chuckled. "Is it not strange how one can misunderstand another for so long? Timon always thought *you* were disapproving of *him*. You frightened us both more than half to death whenever we were forced to deal with you. Now you say it is because you were afraid of your son?"

"Oh, not afraid *of* him. I didn't mean *that.*"

"Then, my lord," she asked, "if you are willing to explain, would you tell us what you did mean?"

"I was afraid *for* him. I was responsible for that tiny mite just as you two are responsible for Francis. Do you mean to say it has never crossed your mind to be afraid for the lad?" he asked his son a trifle belligerently.

Timon grinned. "From the moment I first saw him in his cradle!" He held out his hand. "Do you suppose, Father, that we might try to do better with each other in future?"

"I don't know . . ." Lord Trenton rubbed his chin. "I saw the oddest-looking crop growing in the three-acre field as we went by. If it's what I think it is . . ."

"Don't you say one word against my mangel-wurzels!" said Timon, glowering.

". . . I want to know how you talked old Hervey into allowing them. I never could . . ."

One brow quirked in the most humorous fashion, and after a moment Timon relaxed. Charity chuckled, and then they were all three laughing.

Thinking it over later, once they'd returned to Mumford Manor, Charity recalled Doctor Macalister telling her that, assuming he could let go his worry and concern, Lord Trenton would live a long and happy life.

"Timon," she said, "I think we must send Dr. Mac a letter thanking him for playing Cupid, do not you?"

"I'll willingly do that, but I will not write one to Sir Ivor! He may have been the ace up your huge Scottish Cupid's sleeve, but I still get jealous whenever I think of the way he looks at you when we go up to town.''

Charity smiled. ''You need not ever again feel that way. The last time we were in London Sir Ivor told me his waiting days are over. The lady he has loved forever and ever has been widowed. She is everything he ever wanted in a wife, and I'm to watch the papers for an announcement. I saw it only this morning, Timon.''

''But it has been three months since we were in town. What has taken the man so long?''

Charity giggled. ''It is Lady McKivern, Timon.''

''But . . .''

''I know. She was only just barely a widow when he told me he meant to wed her, so it is surprising it is *only* three months, is it not?''

''McKivern was a nasty old man, but he is gone now. I wish her the best with her rake, but still, Charity, I do not want the man smiling at you with those sad eyes of his!''

''I only want you smiling at me, Timon. And *not* with sadness in your eyes.''

''Good. Smile for me, my love?''

And she did. For many a long and happy year.

LOOK FOR THESE REGENCY ROMANCES

FROM ROSANNE BITTNER:
ZEBRA SAVAGE DESTINY ROMANCE!

#1: SWEET PRAIRIE PASSION   (0-8217-5342-8, $5.99)

#2: RIDE THE FREE WIND   (0-8217-5343-6, $5.99)

#3: RIVER OF LOVE   (0-8217-5344-4, $5.99)

#4: EMBRACE THE
    WILD WIND   (0-8217-5413-0, $5.99)

#7: EAGLE'S SONG   (0-8217-5326-6, $5.99)

PASSIONATE ROMANCE
FROM BETINA KRAHN!

HIDDEN FIRES   (0-8217-4953-6, $4.99)

LOVE'S BRAZEN FIRE   (0-8217-5691-5, $5.99)

MIDNIGHT MAGIC   (0-8217-4994-3, $4.99)

PASSION'S RANSOM   (0-8217-5130-1, $5.99)

REBEL PASSION   (0-8217-5526-9, $5.99)

Available wherever paperbacks are sold, or order direct from the Publisher. Send cover price plus 50¢ per copy for mailing and handling to Kensington Publishing Corp., Consumer Orders, or call (toll free) 888-345-BOOK, to place your order using Mastercard or Visa. Residents of New York and Tennessee must include sales tax. DO NOT SEND CASH.